If you want to be on our confidential mailing list for our Readers' Club Magazine (with extracts from past and forthcoming titles) write to:

SILVER MOON READER SERVICES

The Shadowline Building
6 Wembley Street
Gainsborough
DN21 2AJ
United Kingdom
or
sales@babash.com

or telephone
01427 816710
(UK office hours only)

NEW AUTHORS WELCOME

Please send submissions to
Silver Moon Books Ltd.
PO Box 5663
Nottingham
NG3 6PJ
or
editor@babash.com

First published 2005 Silver Moon Books
ISBN 1-903687-61-6
© 2005 Kim Knight

Unchained 3

Chains That Bind

By

Kim Knight

Also By Kim Knight
Dark Surrender
A Slave's Desire

THIS IS FICTION - IN REAL LIFE ALWAYS PRACTISE SAFE SEX!

PART 1

PROLOGUE:

EIGHT YEARS PREVIOUSLY

He studied her carefully, making sure that the light glinted, just right, off her sweat soaked skin. He moved a little closer and lifted a tendril of soaking, black hair away from her face. His eyes lingered on her rounded breasts and he licked his lips. Her skin was young and smooth, virginal. She was over twenty but it was as if her body hadn't lived - until now.

'Look up,' he said as he backed away to stand behind the tripod-mounted camera. 'I said look up!' he yelled angrily.

She raised her head slowly, her wet hair falling around her shoulders and sticking to her arms that were stretched painfully over her head, bound at the wrist and fixed to a large metal hook hanging from the barn's central beam. Her eyes were red rimmed from constant crying, her cheeks flushed, lips pale. 'Please.' she whispered.

'Shut up,' he snarled as he lowered his eye to the camera, 'Now … look into the camera and just say what I told you.'

She swallowed, desperate to remember what he had made her learn. Her nipples, red and bruised, still ached from where he had pinched them painfully when she had forgotten any of the words. There was a click and he waved for her to start. She swallowed again and then the practised words fell from her trembling lips, 'Mum, dad, you have to listen carefully. Do not call the police. Do not tell anyone. You will have a list of demands with

5

this tape and you must follow every one of them to the letter. There are people watching you to make sure that you behave. Please do as he says or he will hurt me again … worse. If you do not pay the money then …' her voice cracked and she gave a small sob before continuing, '… then you will never see me again and I will be his slave forever.' Her voice broke again and large tears rolled down her cheeks, 'Please, do as he says. Please.'

A click and he raised his eye slowly, studying the hanging woman with a stare that she had become horribly familiar with. He continued to watch her as he turned the camera to face the other direction.

The hanging woman followed his stare and she felt a guilty sense of relief as his lustful stare left her.

On the floor a few feet away was a rectangular hay bale. Fixed over that bale, by means of harsh rope and metal links on the floor, was a younger, naked girl, perhaps eighteen years old. Her head was hanging between her outstretched arms, her breasts crushed and scratched by the straw. Her legs were stretched back and spread, her buttocks slightly raised and glowing red beneath the harsh light.

He started the tape again and then slowly approached the tied girl. She heard him approach and half raised her head. Her lips trembled with fear as she watched him slip the belt from the waist of is trousers. He looped the buckled end around his hand and then raised the strap of leather to shoulder height. She tensed, trembling in fearful anticipation before he brought the belt slicing down across the middle of her buttocks. Her head flew back, her thighs quivering as she cried out, her wrists yanking against the rope that circled them. He lashed her again, the leather slicing down where he had hit her before. He struck her several more times, delivering the strap to the same place over and over again until, with a

6

cry of triumph, he drew blood from her quivering buttocks. He threw the belt away and quickly dropped his trousers, moving between her spread legs.

The hanging woman wanted to close her eyes but she couldn't - she couldn't even blink. All she could do was stare, wide eyed, as he drove himself into the poor girl who cried out and tossed her head. He fucked her violently, his fingernails clawing at the bloodied line and other welts that lined her buttocks. He groaned over and over and then he turned to look at the hanging woman and she knew then, with a terrible sickness in the pit of her stomach, that she was next.

CHAPTER 1.1:

The brand on her buttock, healed now through the passage of time, burned as if freshly singed into her flesh as the sound of her Mistress' footsteps grew louder. The scar was like a beacon, getting hotter with each footfall, heralding her Mistress' approach. Likewise, the clamps on her nipples seemed to tighten of their own accord. She had been bound to the thick wooden pole, her arms and legs wrapped around the woody girth. She remembered that this had been her position when the burning brand had been applied to her buttock, when the lines had been embedded on her skin forever. Permanently marking her with the letter F. Then, as now, her pussy was moist against the harsh pole - her pussy lips having been spread to ensure that her cunt kissed the wood.

She rested her head against the pole and felt beads of sweat rolling down her spine as the footsteps stopped.

The silence was awful. The lack of action even worse.

When the first blow came the anticipation, that had grown during the long minutes, served to heighten the sting. She cried out - as much in surprise as pain and as much in relief that the beating had begun and the terrible wait was over. Her relief was soon forgotten amidst the merciless beating. The ridge of braided leather sliced her buttocks and lower back over and over. Careful twisting s of her Mistress' wrist sent the crop slicing across the curve where her thighs met her buttocks or to find the outer swell of her squashed breasts.

Her Mistress didn't speak - she didn't need to - the message was clear: 'You should never have betrayed me by escaping.'

She sobbed as the message was seared into her very flesh by the torrent of vicious blows. But that wasn't the only message that was silently conveyed.

When the terrible beating finally ended, Natalie sobbed with relief and sorrow. But then suddenly she felt small rubber beads pressing at her anus. The string of anal beads was rammed forcibly into her tight hole, making her gasp and swoon with pleasure. And then her Mistress' fingers were forcing their way towards her cunt and Natalie was coming hard and fast. Her orgasm racked her body as the second silent message filled every fibre of her being; 'You could never truly leave me - I own you and you need me. Your lust and desire form the links in the chains that bind you to me.'

Suddenly she was free from the pole - flat on her back with her knees against her shoulders, her thighs parted and her Mistress' tongue buried deep in her pussy ...

... Natalie awoke with a small cry, gasping as she felt the moisture between her thighs. Beside her, her lover - Mel - stirred within her own dreams. Silently Natalie dipped her fingers to the musky dampness and surrendered herself as easily and as completely as she had surrendered to Faith in her dream, only this time it was her desire that painfully tightened her nipples and anus, chaining her with lust. She gave a small cry in the darkness, too lost in her pleasure to hear another faint cry echoing through the darkened flat.

The cry echoed in the shadows of the bedroom further down the hall, emitted from the lips of the woman who suddenly sat upright, beads of sweat rolling between her naked breasts. Her shaking hand fumbled for the light and once it had been snapped on, she searched every corner and shadow of the room with wide, fearful eyes. As the fretful seconds passed the dream slowly faded and she whispered, 'Faith.' The sound of that name was loud in her ears and drove the last of the dream from her mind.

Giving a ragged sigh, Claudia swung her legs out of bed and sat for a moment, her head resting in her still shaking hands. Eventually she stood up and threw a dressing gown around her naked shoulders before moving towards the door. As she pulled it open she glanced at the clock, 02:17. With a sigh she stepped out and walked quietly down the hall towards the bathroom. She passed the two bedrooms that currently housed the three houseguests - Phoebe in the first room and Mel and Natalie in the second. As she passed the second door she thought that she heard a stifled gasp but paid it no heed.

The bathroom beckoned and once inside she slipped the dressing gown from her shoulders as she pushed the door closed with her hip. She left the gown in a pool of material just inside the door and stepped towards the separate shower unit. She opened the clear glass door and stepped inside, turning the shower jet on to its harshest setting. The hot droplets pounded her skin and she rubbed the sweat away with a sponge. She felt the water trickling down her back and she shivered involuntarily as the water prickled the thin lines that striped her lower back. The scars seemed to come to life beneath the running water. It felt as if a thousand tiny fingers were pinching at her skin, digging thin needles into her flesh. She gasped, swallowed water and choked. She stood with her hands against the white tiles while her shoulders heaved and she tried desperately to regain her breath.

'Damn it.' she cursed and angrily turned the shower off. She ran her hands over her hair, forcing the water to the ends of the glistening, ebony strands. She pushed the cubicle door open and stepped out. Dripping and naked, she turned to close the door.

'Oh god, I'm sorry.'

Claudia gasped and turned as a startled female voice filled the bathroom. She glanced quickly at Natalie and then bent to retrieve her gown. Natalie's opening of the door had moved the gown towards Claudia and as she took a step forward and bent to grab it, she suddenly realised that the neon lighting would be glaring off her back. Mumbling a curse she straightened quickly and moved back, holding her gown to her chest. She looked at Natalie, hoping against hope that the ex-slave had averted her eyes but as they stared at each other she realised that the damage had been done - she had seen everything.

Claudia took a deep breath and as she did so she smelt a musky scent. She must have shown some sort of reaction because Natalie glanced down at her hand that was sticky with her spent juices. As she did so she noticed Claudia follow her line of sight.

A guilty look flashed across Natalie's face and she knew that Claudia had seen that too.

'Is Mel okay?' Claudia asked.

For the briefest of moments Natalie considered lying but then she sighed and replied, 'She's sleeping.'

Claudia threw her gown around her shoulders and tied it securely at the waist. 'Coffee?' Without waiting for an answer, Claudia walked past Natalie, closing the door behind her.

As she quickly washed, Natalie found herself thinking about the enigmatic, raven haired woman. Claudia had recently helped Mel, a freed slave and Natalie's lover, to track her down to a slave-camp in Algeria where Natalie's mistress Faith had sent her to be broken. Once there Claudia had secured her release and the release of another slave, Phoebe. Upon their return to England, Claudia had suggested that they stay at her apartment until they settled into their new, free, lives. And she had done it all without complaint and with no hint that she wanted anything in return. Natalie had been suspicious at first but Mel had eventually convinced her that Claudia, truly, wanted nothing in return. But neither did she offer any suggestion as to her motivation for such apparent altruism. Natalie found this difficult to handle at first but as the days stretched into weeks the issue of Claudia's motivation disappeared into the background, hidden under Natalie's recurring dreams about Faith. Natalie loved Mel above all else and now that they both had their freedom it was everything that they had ever wished for - but Natalie couldn't hide from her inner demon forever, she couldn't deny that darkness within her. For now those dark desires were sated by her dreams but she knew, with a terrible certainty, that those dreams would not feed her hunger for much longer. Her lust and desires were growing despite Mel's affectionate attentions. Mel pleasured her so wonderfully, so tenderly but sometimes … sometimes that hunger gnawed at her gut and in the depths of her pleasure she wished that Mel would hurt her. Just the thought of a cane or crop striking her skin was like a jolt of electricity through her body. She had felt binds at her wrists, breasts and ankles so often that it was easy to feel them again even as Mel nuzzled between her quivering thighs. And it was the memories, increasingly more than Mel's attentions, which brought her to a shuddering climax.

She stared at her reflection as she washed her hands yet again. It was strange, when she was a slave she had always known who she was looking at in the mirror. She had no secrets then, least of all from herself, but now … she stared into the eyes of a stranger. Where did a freed slave really belong? She shook her head violently and stared at her reflection again, forcing herself to recognise her own face. She turned from the mirror before she could see the angry curl of her lip.

Leaving the bathroom, she headed for the kitchen where Claudia was standing by the sink, her shoulders hunched and her knuckles white where she gripped the edge. She must have heard Natalie enter the kitchen because she half turned, her shoulders relaxing. And then, as they stared at each other, for just a second Natalie recognised herself in Claudia more than she had recognised her own reflection a few moments ago. But then the moment passed and Claudia broke the contact as she turned to grab the kettle.

Natalie sat at the kitchen table and watched in silence as Claudia made them both a coffee. There was a packet of cigarettes on the table. She hadn't known that Claudia smoked and had only started smoking again herself a few days ago. She opened the packet and lit one, breathing the smoke deep into her lungs and letting it out as a sigh. Claudia half turned, raising her eyebrow quizzically but she didn't speak.

Natalie had almost finished the cigarette when Claudia approached the table a few minutes later and placed a mug in front of her. 'Thanks.' Natalie said with a vague smile and turned her head to the side as she blew out smoke.

Claudia sat opposite, sliding her chair closer to the table and reaching for the packet. 'So, you couldn't sleep tonight either?' she asked after she had lit one.

Natalie shook her head, 'It's the same thing every night... I can't stop dreaming about her.'

'Faith,' Claudia sighed with a nod.

'You know her, don't you?'

'Yes,' Claudia replied, she had hinted as much when she had first seen the brand on Natalie's buttock but had said nothing further at the time or since.

Natalie took a small breath, 'Was she your ...' the word

caught in her throat, as if saying it would somehow make the young, powerful woman appear. She coughed and tried again, 'Was she your ... Mistress?'

'No,' Claudia replied with a slow shake of her head. She took a deep breath, 'We were lovers.'

Natalie was stunned and it clearly showed in her wide-eyed expression. That shock turned quickly to suspicion, anger and then fear. 'Why didn't you tell us?'

'Because it would mean explaining everything.'

'You don't have to explain anything to me,' Natalie responded with hooded eyes.

'If I don't you'll never trust me.'

Natalie shrugged but didn't reply.

'All right then ...' Claudia sat back and her eyes took on a distance look as if she was looking at something far away, 'It was eight years ago that we met in a seedy bar in Soho.' Claudia noticed the look that flashed across Natalie's eyes, 'It's not quite as bad as it sounds. I had been taken there by my then boyfriend who was desperate to add some spice to our relationship.' ...

... The heavy atmosphere, thick with cigarette smoke, rolled out towards her as Michael opened the door. Without waiting for her, he stepped through into the dark club, not bothering to check if she was following. Claudia Ellis found herself wondering, perhaps for the hundredth time, why she bothered putting up with him. Michael was a working class wide-boy as, no doubt, her parents would call him. That description wasn't definitely true, although it did fully capture the aura of danger that he carried with him. Perhaps that was the attraction. Most of the men that she had ever met, many of whom had been selected by her parents based on the young man's parentage, were all steady, reliable, safe and above all, upper class. Michael was just the opposite and to the young, naive Claudia, that was a potent mix. And besides, he was a stallion in the bedroom. No man had ever made her feel like he did. She hadn't exactly slept around, mostly it was drunken fumblings at university, but none of those men had pleasured her fully. But Michael, he certainly knew how to make her feel good - even if he didn't quite reach that something deep inside her.

She followed him to the bar, sticking close to him for fear that she would be lost within the shadows of the club. She could hear soft voices but couldn't see anyone else and she imagined a dozen pairs of eyes staring out at her from those dark areas around the edges of the large dance floor. She studied the dance floor and the seven or more shining poles that were fixed to the floor and stretched upwards to disappear into the shadows above.

'You want your usual?' Michael asked without looking at her.

Claudia nodded, half turning towards the dance floor as five spotlights suddenly flared into life and a heavy beat rang out from hidden speakers.

Michael ordered their drinks from the barman and then turned as a young, scantily dressed woman appeared from the shadows at the edge of the dance floor. She moved from one pole to the next, twirling and dancing in time to the rhythm. When she completed a circuit she moved to the centre of the floor and removed her bra with a flourish.

'Yeah!' Michael yelled, 'Now that's what I'm talking about!'

The dancer glanced in his direction and cupped her breasts in both hands, squeezing them together and rolling the nipples between thumb and forefinger. She gave him a faint smile and then continued with her routine.

Michael laughed and slipped his arm around Claudia's

shoulders, allowing his hand to lie over her breast. 'That's one hell of a piece of arse, eh?' he laughed and squeezed her breast.

Claudia yelped and pushed him away, 'Don't do that!'

He shrugged and turned to the bar, picking up his drink and tossing it back. 'Put another in there.'

'You haven't paid for those yet,' the barman responded.

Michael stared at him, 'Run me a tab.'

The barman raised an eyebrow and stared at Michael with disdain.

'Alright, alright,' he yanked his wallet from his trousers and handed several notes to the barman. 'That should cover the night's activities. Happy?'

'Ecstatic,' the barman replied as he turned and headed for the till.

'Jumped up little twat,' Michael mumbled.

Claudia took his arm, 'Let's just go. Take me home.'

He stared at her, 'Don't you like it here, baby?'

'No, I don't,' she glanced at the dancer who was slowly removing her panties.

Michael was also watching and he grinned, 'You need to loosen up, baby.'

'Please, Michael, just take me home.'

He sighed, 'Alright, but can I at least finish my drink?'

Claudia nodded.

'Thank you,' he said and snatched up his glass. He lifted himself onto a stool and faced the dance floor. When Michael finished his drink he ordered another and then another.

'Michael,' Claudia sighed as he turned to order yet another drink.

'Oh, come on, babe,' he smiled disarmingly. 'The manager is a friend of mine, he'll be here soon - you'll like him.'

As if on cue a suited man suddenly appeared from

behind a curtain on the opposite side of the bar.

'Michael!' the overweight man greeted him happily, extending his hand over the bar. 'Is this business or pleasure?'

'Pleasure,' Michael replied warmly, half glancing at Claudia, 'Stuart, this is my girlfriend Claudia.'

The club manager studied her for a few seconds longer than necessary before smiling, 'Very pretty.' He poured himself a drink and then moved round the bar. 'Shall we?' he invited and directed towards a table.

As they sat at the shadowed table a new dancer appeared. She was younger than the first and smaller in all proportions but, and Claudia was surprised to realise her own interest, this new dancer was far more attractive. Her dark curls bounced around her face and shoulders and she demonstrated an incredible athleticism and strength as she lifted herself up the poles and spun around them. She was a delight to watch, her movements fluid and natural. She reminded Claudia of the dancers at the ballets that her parents had taken her to see regularly when she was growing up. Claudia was so entranced with her dancing that she didn't even notice when she started to undress.

'Nice pert tits,' Michael announced suddenly and Claudia realised, for the first time, that the young woman was now completely naked. She quickly looked away, relieved to realise that both men had been too engrossed in the performance to notice her avid attention.

Claudia heard Stuart shout something but couldn't make out what he said. The dancer turned and Claudia swallowed nervously when she realised that Stuart had called her over. The dancer reached the table, glancing briefly at Claudia and revealing eyes that were almost black in the darkness. The dancer turned her attention to Michael, 'You like what you see, honey?'

'You bet I do,' he replied and slapped her buttocks.

'Hey, watch it!' the dancer yelled, looking at Stuart for support, 'There's a no touching rule here.'

Stuart waved his hand dismissively, 'Mike's a friend, we can skip the rules.'

A look of anger flashed across her face but she didn't say anything as Michael pulled her down onto the seat between him and Claudia. Michael's hand slapped down on her naked thigh and then his other hand reached for her breast.

Claudia stood up, 'I'm going home.'

Michael reached across and grabbed her arm, pulling her back down, 'Be patient, darling, you can have a play next.'

Claudia was too stunned to respond and could only sit and stare as Michael made the dancer stand and lean over the table. He ran his hands over the mounds of her buttocks, grinning madly to himself as he parted the smooth cheeks to reveal the star of her anus and the cleft of her pussy.

'Oh man, I wanna stick my cock up your arse,' he announced, slapping her buttocks with both hands.

Stuart laughed and then excused himself as the barman beckoned him.

Michael slapped her buttocks again and then slowly dragged his thumb down between her buttocks. 'Maybe I'll get my girl to sit on your face while I fuck you.'

'That's it,' Claudia announced furiously and stood up, 'Goodbye, Michael.' She moved around the table but Michael jumped up and moved around the other way to block her exit.

'Where are you going?' he demanded.

'Home,' she replied.'And don't bother trying to come with me, you stay here and have your fun.'

'But I want you to watch,' Michael smiled.

Claudia was stunned. 'Don't be so vile.'

'You frigid little tart!' Michael was furious that his plans had been ruined, 'All I wanted was a bit of fun.'

'Well, you can have as much fun as you want - we're finished,' she responded.

'I say when we're finished,' he said and grabbed her arm but she shook him off.

'Goodbye, Michael.'

She turned but he suddenly grabbed her hair and threw her across the table. Glasses flew from under her and, unable to steady herself, she rolled onto the floor. Michael moved in on her, grabbing the front of her blouse and hauling her up so that he could slap her harshly. Claudia cried out, raising her hands to protect herself as Michael prepared to hit her again. Then, suddenly, Michael was being dragged off her and she heard him yelp with pain. She looked up and saw the naked dancer glaring at Michael, her fingers curled into a claw.

'Leave her alone,' the dancer said quietly, menacingly.

'You fucking bitch!' Michael snarled as he prodded at the four bloody scratches on his cheek.

The dancer bent to help Claudia to her feet as Michael stared at the tips of his fingers that glinted darkly with specks of blood. With a growl of fury, Michael stepped towards the dancer who stepped back and slashed at his face again, narrowly missing his eyes. Hands suddenly grabbed her and hauled the dancer away. Claudia turned to see that it was the manager, Stuart, who held the dancer back.

'What the fuck is this?' Michael demanded of Stuart.

'I'll deal with it,' Stuart responded quickly. 'I'm very sorry.'

Before Claudia could protest, Stuart had dragged the dancer away.

'Get me another fucking drink!' Michael yelled to the

barman. He slumped down on the seat and prodded the scratches on his cheek. 'Fuck,' he cursed angrily.

'You're staying?' Claudia asked, her voice cracked with emotion.

'Yeah, looks like it.'

'Well, I'm going.'

'Fuck off then, 'cos you're no fucking fun. Stuck up fucking rich kid.'

Claudia stared at him, tears stinging her eyes.

He looked up at her, 'You still here?'

She gave a small sob and then turned and fled the club … … 'Faith was the dancer?' Natalie asked, her voice betraying her surprise. It was hard to imagine Faith in any role other than that of the sadistic mistress who had abused and manipulated Natalie before burning her initial into her flesh, marking her forever.

Claudia nodded slowly. 'Not exactly love at first sight, but she made a lasting impression that night.' She stood up, taking her cup with her. After pouring the dregs of the coffee down the sink, she turned and leant against the enamel.

'What happened with the guy? Michael?'

'What can I say?' Claudia sighed, 'I was young and naive and Michael's opinion really mattered to me. He came to my apartment a few days later, carrying a huge bunch of roses and a humble apology.'

'And you forgave him?'

Claudia nodded, as her eyes grew distant …

… Twenty-one red roses lay scattered around the living room, along with various items of clothing. On the sofa Claudia gasped and ground herself down onto Michael's cock as he held her buttocks in his large hands. He thrust up to meet her downward push and she gasped again, burying her head in his shoulder. His teeth found the sensitive skin at her neck and he nibbled softly. His hands parted her buttocks, his thumb rubbing over the star of her anus. She wanted to pull away, to tell him that she didn't want that - but she was too far gone and the thought of just letting him have his way sent a new warmth to her groin. She tensed as the tip of his thumb pushed against the resistance of her anus. She groaned and then gave a small cry as the thick digit entered her, going in as far as the first knuckle. Michael thrust up harshly, his own passions mounting. Claudia rode with him, crying out as he raked his free hand down her back, scratching her skin. In the midst of her rising climax, the stinging of his nails was electric and she cried out, grinding down harder on his cock. Suddenly he yanked his thumb free of her arse and slapped both hands onto her buttocks. The burning sting of the blow turned quickly to a wave of ice that rolled up her back and down her chest, making her scream loudly as she climaxed. Her spasming pussy clenched his cock and he growled at his own climax and shot his come deep into her.

She stayed on top of him, panting breathlessly, for several moments until he said, 'You'll have to get off, I've got to go, babe.'

Sighing, she climbed off his lap and quickly found her panties. Michael dressed quickly, barely looking at her.

'You only just got here,' she grumbled.

'Yeah, sorry, babe.' He managed a smile, 'Are you in tonight?'

She nodded and smiled hopefully, 'I'll see you then?'

'Nah, I told you, I'm meeting a contact with regards to a big deal.' He tied his shoelaces, kissed her on the cheek and headed for the door. He was about to open it when he paused and glanced over his shoulder, 'Your parents still living in Regents Square?'

Claudia nodded, grimacing - she hated it when he

21

spoke about her parents, it usually led to some sort of remark about her coming from money, silver spoon up the arse and such like.

'Right.' He turned for the door.

'Why?'

'No reason.' He opened the door and stepped out, not looking back as it closed behind him.

A half an hour later and Claudia was just stepping into the shower when there was a knock at the door. Thinking it was Michael, she threw a gown loosely around her shoulders and hurried to answer it. Smiling, she pulled the door open. 'Did you manage to cancel your -' she stopped, her mouth hanging open as she stared at her visitor.

'I have to talk to you.'

Claudia was too stunned to react immediately and the dancer from the club pushed past.

'You gonna close the door?' the dancer asked and strolled into the living room.

Claudia quickly closed the door and hurried after her. She found the dancer idly stroking the roses that Claudia had arranged in a crystal vase.

'Nice place you have here,' she looked over her shoulder at Claudia, 'I'm Faith.'

Claudia stared at her, waiting for some sort of explanation.

'I have to talk to you.'

'How did you find me?' Claudia asked, no longer content to wait for answers.

'I don't have time to explain.'

Claudia didn't believe that - it seemed more likely that the young woman was reluctant to tell her. It didn't matter - Claudia had more immediate concerns.

'Why are you here?'

'I need money.'

'What?' Claudia was aghast at the young woman's bluntness.

'I'm sorry but I know you can help me - I have to get out of this city.' Faith responded, 'And maybe you should do the same.'

'Why?'

'Because that boyfriend of yours is dangerous.'

Claudia shook her head, 'He apologised for the other night, he was just drunk.'

'Well, I guess everything is okay then,' Faith snarled. 'He slaps you about, apologises and then you forgive him. We should all have such luxuries.'

Claudia replayed the night's events quickly in her mind. 'Did the manager, Stuart, hurt you?'

Faith stared at her blankly, 'What do you think?'

Claudia sighed, she felt sorry for the young woman but she wasn't her responsibility. 'Look, I appreciate that you tried to help me and I'm sorry that you got into trouble - but I'm not in the habit of giving money to …' she paused and Faith jumped in angrily.

'To who? Whores? Slappers? Bitches like me who could wave their tits in your boyfriend's face and make him come in his pants without even touching him?'

'I was going to say … to strangers. But thanks for helping me make up my mind.' Claudia turned and headed for the front door, holding it open and staring pointedly at Faith.

Faith walked slowly towards the door. She stepped out and half turned to Claudia, 'Just do me a favour, eh? Dump that wanker of a boyfriend before he hurts you again.'

'Thanks for the advice,' Claudia responded flatly and pushed the door closed.

That evening Claudia ordered herself a meal from an expensive restaurant and ate it on her lap in front of the

TV - her mother would have thrown a fit to see her. She had another shower and then went to bed.

She awoke with a start. Something was wrong. She moved to swing her legs out of bed but she was suddenly grabbed and thrown back onto the mattress. Something glinted and she caught sight of a knife.

'Fight back and I will cut you up. Understand?'

Claudia nodded slowly, staring into the blue eyes that stared out from behind the woollen mask.

'What the hell is going on?' she thought, adrenalin overriding her fear for the time being. Something fell into her lap and she recognised the outline of her car keys.

'Time to go, sweet thing,' he grabbed her arm and she allowed herself to be led from the flat.

Everything had happened so fast that she was having trouble keeping up. Suddenly they were downstairs and out on the street. She saw her car a little further down the street and her keys felt like a lead weight in her hand. She knew that she had to fight him but she could neither drop the keys nor lift her hands, the adrenalin had faded leaving her with only strength-sapping fear. If she couldn't fight, then she could shout. She opened her mouth to scream.

'Get away from her!'

She heard the vaguely familiar female voice and then there was grunt and the sound of a body hitting the floor. Claudia looked down, stunned to see her assailant lying prone on the pavement. She cried out as a hand gripped her arm. She found the strength to fight back and lashed out with the car keys.

'Watch it!'

'Faith?' Claudia frowned, her fear numbed brain slowly working out that it was the dancer who had saved her.

'Yeah. Now can we -'

Claudia jumped back as Faith gasped and fell towards her, collapsing to the pavement and revealing a second masked man. Claudia tried to scream but his hand slapped her mouth into silence. She was dragged to her car and forced into the driving seat, held there by the second assailant and a knife. The unconscious Faith was thrown into the back seat by the first attacker who had regained enough of his senses.

'Off we go then., the masked man in the back growled, a laugh rolling from his throat.

The point of the knife dug into her throat and she quickly started the engine …

… 'It was nearly dawn when he told me to stop," Claudia continued, her eyes watching Natalie's cigarette smoke curl lazilily up from the ashtray. 'Faith was still unconscious in the back of the car. I pulled on the handbrake and … that's the last thing I remember.' Claudia stared at her hands, 'The second guy wasn't there when I woke up which was probably for the best because the guy who had grabbed me did enough all by himself.'
…

… There was no gradual return. No slow, fuzzy return to full consciousness. There was just the darkness and then there was the harsh light. She had to squint against the glare that stung and brought tears to her eyes. The harsh light was enough of a jolt to bring her memories back as quickly as her consciousness. Almost straight away she remembered what had happened and just as quickly, she was terrified. She tried to force the fear down, swallowing it into the pit of her stomach. She had a clear idea that her fear would be of no help to her now.

Her vision gradually cleared and she realised, as more of her senses returned, that she was upright. She tried to move and gave a small cry as her wrists burned and her arms threatened to dislodge from their sockets. There was a jangling from above her and she knew that she was chained. She tried to look up and managed to see coils of harsh rope wrapped around her wrists, holding them together. That rope was attached to a chain and somewhere above, she could vaguely make out a large metal hook and a wooden beam.

Something moved in the light and a moment later the white glare retreated a little as if the light had been moved from her eyes. She blinked, trying to clear the tears and to get her eyes to adjust. When she could see again the sight of a man, stripped to the waist, greeted her, he wore nothing but a pair of tight leather pants that hugged his legs. He was neither fat nor muscular and his body was pale and hairless, save for the close-cropped dark hair atop his head. His face was expressionless, blank and empty, but his eyes danced with lust and desire. Claudia had to look away from that gaze, finding his eyes harder to look at than the white glare of the photographer's lamp that stood to his right. As she looked down her eyes took in the length of her own naked body and she felt that fear in her stomach rise up her throat. She fought down the urge to scream for help, reasoning that there was probably little point. She managed to look back at the man but avoided his eyes, choosing instead to focus on a small white scar on his upper lip.

'What do you want?' she sounded scared and she hated herself for it.

He didn't answer, he just smiled. The smile was the same as the look in his eyes and Claudia swallowed.

'Where's the girl who was with me?' she asked, suddenly remembering Faith.

The smile widened a little as the man slowly stepped sideways and Claudia took a sharp intake of breath. Behind the man was a large, rectangular hay-bale, bound with lines of blue rope. On her knees, lying over that bale, naked and shining with perspiration, was Faith. Her arms had been stretched out over the bale and handcuffs, which had been fixed to the rope, held her wrists. She had her cheek resting on the hay, her eyes open and staring at Claudia. Something had been shoved into her mouth as a gag and her cheeks puffed as she tried to breathe.

'Is she all right?'

The man tipped his head slightly to the side, studying Claudia in silence. After an eternity he slowly stepped backwards until he was standing at Faith's feet. He turned and then, from behind his back, he withdrew a long riding crop. He raised the crop and watched Claudia carefully as he brought the whip slicing down across Faith's raised buttocks. Faith jumped beneath the blow, her arms wrenching against the cuffs as her body quivered. Her cry was muffled behind the gag. Claudia's cry wasn't muffled and it rang out as the chains above her jangled.

'What are you doing?' she cried.

The crop landed again. Flattening Faith's buttocks and sending tiny droplets of sweat into the air. He delivered several more blows, raising harsh red welts across the smooth mounds. The sound of brutal snaps echoed around the barn and rang in Claudia's ears as tears streaked her cheeks. Faith had turned her face so that her forehead was resting against the bale and although Claudia couldn't see her features, the quivering of Faith's shoulders was enough for her to know that Faith was crying.

The man cast the crop aside, watching Claudia intently as he slowly began to unfasten his trousers. His intent was clear and Claudia sobbed out loud. 'Please, don't.' she whispered and knew that he had heard her because to his smile widened as he lowered himself to his knees between Faith's legs. His thick fingers parted her

27

buttocks and she tensed as his grip pressed against the fresh welts. His hardened cock pressed at her entrance and, with a groan from Faith, he slid into her tight passage. His fingernails dug into the welts and Faith threw her head back, her eyes screwed tightly shut as he slammed into her. He fucked her hard but slowly, his thighs slamming against the back of Faith's legs with every thrust. And with every thrust, he studied Claudia's reaction. Claudia couldn't tear her eyes from the scene, as much as she wanted to. Her only respite was the tears that misted her vision, blurring some of the details of his deliberately hard fucking. It was several minutes before he picked up the pace of his screwing and began to hammer Faith's pussy with even harder, faster thrusts. Suddenly he groaned and pulled free of her bruised pussy, clamping his cock into one hand he aimed his jet of semen at her reddened buttocks, gasping as he came. Then, with a small laugh, he used his large palms to rub the salty mix into the welts. Faith tensed, her wrists pulled at the handcuffs as she tried to pull away. But she had nowhere to go and had to suffer further.

When he was done he approached Claudia and stood less than a foot in front of her. Slowly he raised his hands and ran his palms down her breasts, smearing them with what was left of his come. Claudia grimaced and tried to pull away but he grabbed her nipples between thumb and forefinger, forcing her to stay still. Once she was still again, he released her nipples and studied the hardness of them. Smiling to himself he reached into his pocket and retrieved a small metal device. Claudia had no idea what it was until he slipped it over the sensitive bud and slowly tightened it. She gasped and then cried out as her nipple was cruelly pinched. He tightened it until it was unbearable. Claudia gasped over and over, gritting her teeth against the biting sting at her breast.

He retrieved another of the clamps and Claudia tried to turn away but he simply dug his nails into her breast and turned her back. Once the second clamp was attached, Claudia hissed through her teeth, fresh tears welling from her eyes.

With the clamps attached he stepped back and studied her, that same smile playing across his lips.

'You're not used to pain, are you?' The question was so sudden, so unexpected, that Claudia didn't answer straight away. His lips curled with anger and he grabbed the nipple clamps, lifting them up and pulling her breasts painfully. 'Answer me.'

'No,' Claudia gasped, trying not to cry out. 'No I'm not used to pain.'

He let go of her breasts and turned to pick up the crop. 'You've never been whipped before, have you?'

She stared at the crop fearfully and shook her head. 'No,' she whispered.

'Your friend has,' he announced.

Claudia stared at Faith and realised that the young woman was watching them, her eyes filled with pain.

'Your friend has been whipped before - she knows pain.' His voice came from behind her, she hadn't realised that he had moved. She almost cried out as he traced the end of the crop down her spine. 'There are little thin scars across her buttocks. Hard to see unless you know what you're looking for.' The end of the crop reached the base of spine and then drew a line across the centre of her buttocks. 'I think she even likes a little pain. I felt her juices on my cock when I was screwing her.'

Faith closed her eyes, fresh tears rolling from behind the closed lids.

The crop was lifted from her skin and instinctively Claudia knew what was going to happen next. She closed her eyes and held her breath. The clamps at her nipples seemed to tighten and her breasts burned all the more as her skin tingled with fearful suspense. She heard the swish of the crop a moment before it found her buttocks. There was a loud snap and for a second it didn't hurt - it felt as if a freezing blanket had been thrown over her skin as her body swayed under the force of the blow. The initial shock passed quickly and Claudia cried out as her buttocks suddenly seared into life with a terrible burning sting, as if a hundred hot needles had been pushed into her flesh. The burning line was crossed by another blow, struck from the other direction and there was no shock this time, just the awful burn and the cry that tore from her throat. She lost count of the blows that landed on her virgin buttocks. Her cries turned to disbelieving screams and then to pleas. Between her cries she begged him to stop but he paid no heed and beat her mercilessly. Her buttocks throbbed with such intensity that the pain soon engulfed her whole body, heightening the ache at her wrists, shoulders and breasts. With every blow of the crop, it felt as if the clamps at her nipples were being tightened. And when she felt as if she could stand no more, he cast the crop aside and kicked her legs apart. His hand slapped up between her legs, his rough fingers searching out the petals of her pussy. The tip of his finger entered her and he pressed at the entrance before sliding the digit in to the first knuckle. The pain-induced adrenalin that coursed through her body heightened every single nerve ending and she sobbed out loud as she felt her pussy react to his touch, as if searching for some escape from the agony of her wounded buttocks and clamped nipples. He pressed himself against her back, sliding another finger into her cunt. She gasped and then sobbed again.

'Please, don't,' she whispered.

He laughed into her hair and forced another two digits

into her vagina. She cried out as he bruised her and then gasped as his probing fingers found that innermost spot. His thumb found her clitoris and her body reacted as if she had suffered an electric shock. He pumped his hand into her, his thumb crushing her clitoris and she cried out, as much in pain as in rejection of her own reaction. She tried to ignore the growing throb at her pussy, the familiar warmth in her abdomen but his fingers continued to ply her pussy with consummate skill and despite her pain, despite her fear, she knew that if he continued she was going to come. She tried to recapture the fear that she had felt when she had first awoken, tried to link that with the pain that he had wrought upon her. She felt her climax edging closer and she cried out in a desperate attempt to shake herself from it. Suddenly his hand reached up to her breast and released the clamp, dropping it to the floor. He did the same with the other side as Claudia cried out. The removal of the clamps had been almost as painful as when they had been out on but the relief to be free of them was intense. That intensity filled her groin and her pussy spasmed, her juices splashing his palm as she threw her head back and screamed …

… 'You climaxed?'

Claudia forced herself to look up at Natalie. She nodded slowly.

'And you've never forgotten that? Never forgiven yourself?'

Claudia sighed and gave a small shrug. She turned to pour herself another coffee.

'You never forget the first time that you succumb.' Natalie sighed, her own eyes growing distant for the briefest of moments. 'But a good Master or Mistress can do that to almost anyone. Even the strongest person can't fight their own body. Pain and pleasure are so closely linked that it doesn't take much to push it either way.'

She looked at Claudia, her eyes focusing again, 'What happened afterwards?'

Claudia sipped her coffee and took a deep breath …

… 'No!' he yelled angrily and Claudia cried out as his finger twisted her bruised nipple, 'Say it again and do it fucking right!'

Claudia sobbed, her mind racing to remember the words that he had told her.

'Say it!' he yelled, snapping his fingers from her breast and slapping her hard across the face.

She sobbed again and then took a deep breath, 'Mum, Dad, you have to listen carefully. Do not call the police, do not tell anyone. You will have a list of instructions with -'

'No! No! No!' he screamed, each word punctuated with a pinch to her nipples. 'Demands you stupid whore, I'm making a fucking demand!' He glared at her, 'I've had you for three fucking days, do you think mummy and daddy are gonna follow instructions? I'm fucking demanding their money and their attention. Demand … do you fucking understand?'

'I'm sorry,' she sobbed, 'please, just give me a little while … I just need a few minutes … please.'

He stared at her, fury dancing in his eyes. 'You want a break, is that it?'

'Yes … oh, please, yes.'

'Yes, what?'

'Yes, Master.'

'Yes, Master, what?'

'Yes, Master, I need a break. Please … Master.'

He studied her in silence. He had hung her from the beam, as he did every time he wanted to beat or fuck her. Today he had wanted her to learn the ransom speech and she had been trying desperately to learn it for the last three hours. He had only told her it once. 'All right.'

he sighed eventually and turned away.

Claudia sighed with relief.

'You can have a break while I play with my slave.'

Claudia stared at him, her lips trembling. She wanted to stop him, to say that she didn't need a break that she could continue but she couldn't continue and Faith would suffer for it.

Faith was once again stretched over the hay-bale. Her wrists were secured to the floor by handcuffs and metal rings. Her hips rested over the bale, her buttocks raised and prominent. Her ankles were tied to identical rings screwed into the wooden barn floor, her legs cruelly stretched apart. He had started to call Faith his slave soon after they had first awoken in the barn and had treated her more harshly then he had Claudia. Claudia was too weak and too scared to argue and she watched in silence as he stepped between Faith's legs and raised the ever-present crop. He lashed her buttocks, slicing the already bruised and terribly marked flesh. He had not gagged her that morning and her cries rang out through the barn. When he had delivered several vicious blows to her buttocks, he turned the crop and sliced at her inner thighs, delivering alternate lashes to either leg. Finally he delivered five stinging blows to her pussy, wringing high-pitched, pitiful cries from her lips.

'Nice and tender,' he laughed as he quickly released his throbbing cock and sank between her swollen pussy lips. He rode her violently for several minutes, his nails digging into her buttocks. When his groans became louder, he abruptly pulled free and moved round so that he was kneeling at Faith's head. Pulling on her hair and raising her head to an awkward angle, he slipped between her lips, forcing himself in as far as he could go. She gagged and tried to pull away but he fucked her mouth until he suddenly pulled back and splashed her face with semen.

He wiped himself clean on her hair and then stood. Moving to where he had left the crop, he plucked it up and approached Claudia, tapping the crop against his palm. 'Now then,' he announced cruelly, 'shall we get this fucking ransom demand right. After all, the sooner the ransom is paid, the sooner you can go home to mummy and daddy.' ...

... Natalie lit a cigarette with shaking hands and studied the other woman who was staring at the empty cup cradled in her hands. She had been able to visualise everything that Claudia had described - it had been easy enough since she had either witnessed or been on the receiving end of similar abuse frequently enough over the past few years. She shifted in her seat and felt her damp panties between her legs. She felt a stirring of guilt in the pit of her stomach although she knew that she needn't have felt guilty. There were few secrets between her and the raven-haired woman. Claudia must have known that her descriptions would have played to Natalie's sexual demons and she seemed unconcerned by it. Natalie remembered what Mel had told her about how they had managed to track her down to that hell-on-earth slave camp in Algeria. Claudia was no stranger to this world and clearly wielded consummate skill as a Mistress. Suddenly Natalie realised that Claudia's story was far from over.

Natalie cleared her throat, 'So ... your parents paid the ransom?'

Claudia looked up slowly and nodded, but there was look in her eyes - sadness, regret. Anger?

Natalie frowned, 'What?'

'The ransom was only for me. Faith was left behind.' Claudia shook her head, 'I didn't realise until after I had been set free. I told my parents but they didn't care.'

Claudia stared at her hands again, 'I couldn't believe it. I told them that we had to find her but they wouldn't listen. They said that they had no responsibility for her. We argued and I've hardly spoken to them since.' Claudia's tone turned from anger to regretful, 'I hired two private detectives to try and find her but they didn't find anything. And then, three months later ...'

... Claudia slammed the phone down, 'Another dead end.'

Michael stared at her, 'Don't you think you're being a bit obsessive with all this?'

'Obsessive?' Claudia cried. 'That young woman is in a really bad place and I'm the only one who seems to care.'

'She's probably enjoying every minute of it,' Michael sighed, stroking his cheek where Faith had scratched him. 'The girl's a slut.'

Claudia stared at him with barely contained fury but Michael didn't notice.

'Stupid whore deserves everything she gets.'

'She was just trying to help me, Michael.'

'Yeah? Well maybe that crack to the back of the head knocked some sense into her.'

Claudia stared at him, her anger turning to ice in the pit of her stomach. Everything had happened so fast that night she was kidnapped that it was hard too put it all into words - so she hadn't given Michael, or anyone else, the full details of what had happened. So how did he know that Faith had been hit over the head? She was about to say something but stopped herself. Michael was still ranting but Claudia barely heard him - all she could hear was Faith's voice, 'That boyfriend of yours is dangerous.' The ice in her stomach grew until it encompassed her entire chest, making her heart feel like a rock slamming against her ribs.

Michael's rant continued for several minutes, by which time Claudia had been able to settle herself enough to keep a calm exterior - while inside her heart and mind were racing. What should she do? Confront him? Go to the police? Each option that she came up with seemed to be more perilous for Faith than the last. Eventually there was only one option left to her and once she had decided upon that course of action her hammering heart eased to a steady thump.

The rest of the afternoon passed and, as early evening approached, Michael announced that he had a business meeting to attend. He gave her a distracted goodbye and then left. Claudia counted to sixty and then followed him. When she reached the street she glanced towards Michael's car. He was sitting in the front seat, rolling a cigarette - as she knew he would be. Walking quickly to her own car she unlocked it and climbed in. As she shrank down behind the wheel she was grateful that she lived in a one-way street and would therefore not have to worry about Michael pulling a u-turn. It was only a few moments later that he started the engine and pulled away from the kerb. Claudia left a fair distance before she followed him, although she doubted that he would see her, given his habit of totally ignoring his mirrors unless he wanted to look at himself. As she followed Michael she found herself wondering what the hell she had ever seen in him. Her ponderings carried her all the way out of the city.

As they drove through the Kent countryside, Claudia occasionally had the sense of a familiar landmark or turning but it was difficult to remember the journey that she had made so many weeks ago.

They drove for perhaps an hour and a half before Michael slowed and turned into a narrow road. As Claudia turned to follow him, the familiarity of the single-track lane hit her like a hammer in the chest. She allowed Michael to disappear around the bend - knowing full well that this lane led to a dilapidated farmhouse and barn. She considered calling the police right there and then; but if she was wrong ... Instead she guided the car to a shadowed lay-by and walked the rest of the way. Michael wasn't in his car and she could see light around the barn door. She approached carefully, desperate not to make a sound. Moving round the side of the barn she found a rotten plank which she could ease to the side to allow her to see inside.

She saw Michael and she saw him - the man who had abused her - and she saw Faith. The vision before her forced its way into her mind, fixing itself there forever. Faith was on her knees, forehead resting on the ground. Her thighs were straight, her buttocks held up so that Michael could sink his cock between them. Her wrists were cuffed and attached to a chain that hung from the beams. The man who had abused them, the man she knew only as him, was thrashing Faith's back with several thin strips of leather.

The breath caught in Claudia's throat and her heart seemed to freeze in her chest. She sank to her knees, her eyes falling from the hole in the barn side - she couldn't breathe but then her body took over and heaved breath into her lungs. She crawled away from the barn and, once at a safe distance, she called the police.

She only remembered tiny portions of the conversation. Hostage ... old barn ... just stay there ... you've given us enough to find you ... just stay there ... do not enter the building ... we're on our way.

Claudia crawled back to the barn and found herself staring back through that gap. They had changed positions. The chain that had held her wrists now held Faith's ankles and she had been hauled up until only her fingertips brushed the floor. Both men were setting about her with the whips made of leather strips. Michael lashed her breasts and the front of her thighs, the other man lashed her buttocks and the back of her thighs. Faith was mumbling incoherently, tears rolling from her eyes and soaking her sweat soaked hair. Her body twisted with each blow but the alternate strikes kept her moving back again. After several minutes the two men stepped back and studied Faith in silence. Frowning, Claudia leant closer to the gap and strained to listen. A feint humming noise echoed from the barn. The source of the noise became clear when Michael forced his fingers between Faith's tight thighs and a moment later Faith cried out and convulsed, as the humming grew louder. Michael stepped back, watching intently as Faith's body continued to quiver violently, her hips bucking back and forth. Faith suddenly screamed, a long, soul-piercing scream and then she completely relaxed. Michael nodded with satisfaction before waving for his companion to let her down. Once she was on the floor he released her ankles and slipped the humming vibrator from her soaking pussy. Michael wiped the juice-smothered phallus across her breasts and then watched with amusement as the other man fell onto her, licking her breasts clean. His passions rose quickly and within moments he had pushed his trousers to his knees and rammed himself between her thighs, making her cry out again as he hammered her bruised, sensitive pussy …

… 'The police arrived eventually.' Claudia lit herself a cigarette, her hands were shaking. 'They got … him … but Michael managed to get away.'

Natalie swallowed, still reeling from the sights that Claudia had described. She reached forward and took a cigarette for herself, lighting it with hands that were also shaking.

'During the days that followed, the police questioning and everything else, Faith and I grew close. She didn't have anywhere to live so I said that she could stay at my flat until everything had died down.' Claudia took a drag on her cigarette, 'By the time everything had died down and I could live my life normally again, Faith and I were lovers.'

Faith. The name rolled around Natalie's mind, pulling at her brain with that nagging fear that always accompanied it. She had listened to Claudia, but still found it difficult to see Faith in the role of victim and slave. Natalie couldn't see Faith as anything but the vicious, powerful Mistress who had manipulated and abused her for days before finally burning her initial into her flesh. No matter what had happened in her past, Faith would always be that Mistress who had sent her to that slave camp to be broken. Natalie couldn't, and wouldn't, see her any other way.

'I understand how you feel.' Claudia said with a nod, perhaps reading the confusion behind Natalie's eyes, 'If it helps - think of her as two separate people. That's what I have to do,' she sighed. 'I can't think of the woman that abused you and see my Faith. I have followed her as best I can for the last six years - the person that she is now, the Mistress Faith - is not the woman I loved. The woman I loved is lost to the past.'

Natalie stared at her, 'Except, that's not quite true, is it? No matter what she does, a part of you will always love her - I can see it in your eyes.'

Claudia looked away, shaking her head.

Natalie wasn't annoyed by Claudia's naivety but she was concerned by it. Mel's Master, Nash, had had very clear ideas about all-consuming love and he had been right. She knew the deep love that Claudia had spoken of, she knew what it was to seek solace in the arms of another. She and Mel had done the very same. Nothing could ever make her dismiss her love of Mel the way that Claudia had tried to dismiss her love of Faith. Nothing was ever that clear-cut.

'Faith embraced that world quicker than I did,' Claudia continued, dragging them both back to the past. 'She started going to clubs and exhibitions. She didn't know that I had seen Michael bring her to climax but I could see that that passion had stayed in her. I don't think that he unlocked that side of Faith's nature, I think that it had already been noticed long before I met her. But Michael and his ... friend ... exposed it completely - to Faith as much as anyone.' Claudia sighed, that same sad sigh that had punctuated her speech throughout. 'I was secure in my relationship with Faith and I felt sure that, when I was ready, I would allow her to show me more.'

Natalie nodded, she understood what Claudia was saying - watching Faith climax under those harsh conditions had unlocked something in Claudia too - but it had exposed a raw nerve that had remained sensitive.

'It was over a year later, things were going well for us. Faith enjoyed her passions whenever and wherever she liked and I felt secure in the knowledge that it was my arms that she came home to.' Claudia took a deep, sad breath, 'And then Michael reappeared ...'

... 'What the fuck do you want?' Claudia demanded and then waved her hand, 'No, forget that.' She moved to close the door but Michael slammed his shoulder against it and pushed it open. Barging past Claudia he ran into the living room. Claudia closed the door and quickly followed. She found Michael at the window, nervously staring out.

'Did you close the door?' Michael asked.

'Yes, but I'll be opening it again in a minute when I throw you out.'

Michael stared at her - he actually seemed shocked that she was angry with him. 'You wouldn't throw me out.'

Claudia stared back, 'No - maybe I could call the police instead.'

He held his hands up, 'Alright, alright, let's just calm down.'

'What the fuck do you want, Michael?'

'I need money.'

Claudia snorted.

'I've got men after me. Bad men.' Michael sounded desperate, 'I need to get out of the country.'

'Why the hell should I help you?'

He thought for a moment before fixing her with an icy, hard stare. 'If you don't, I'll have to find the money some other way. I heard you shacked up with that whore - I bet her old boss would pay a pretty penny to get her back.'

'Leave her out of this.'

'Gladly. Give me the money I need and I will be out of your life forever.'

Claudia took a deep breath and slowly nodded, 'How much do you need?'

He told her.

'Alright.' Claudia realised that Michael was smart enough to ask for an amount that he knew Claudia could get her hands on quickly. 'I can give you half in cash and the rest in bits and pieces that you can sell.'

Michael nodded, 'That'll do.'

She glared at him - not even a thank-you slipped from his lips. She rounded everything up and almost threw it at him. 'Now - get out of my life.'

He smiled leeringly at her, 'Not even a fuck for old times sake? I could force you - I reckon you'd like that.'

Claudia moved for the phone, 'The next thing I'll do

is call the police.'

'Goodbye, sweetheart.' Michael sneered and headed for the door.

Once the door had closed behind him Claudia sank onto the sofa and held her head in her shaking hands. It was only a matter of minutes before she heard the front door opening. She smiled to herself, Faith was home, a friendly face to settle her nerves and anger.

'Hi, babe,' she looked towards the door but there was no friendly face there. What she saw was the face of a stranger.

'Guess who I just bumped into,' the words dripped with fury as Faith stood, staring coldly at Claudia. Claudia swallowed, suddenly more afraid of Faith than she had ever been of Michael …

… Claudia blinked and wiped her eyes. 'She left me the next day. She took money from my bank account and bought herself a new life.'

Natalie stared at her, frowning, and then the meaning behind Claudia's words slowly sank in. 'She paid her way back in - she paid her way in and became a Mistress,' Natalie breathed.

Claudia nodded, 'I left it all for a while, tried to forget about it. I took myself off on holiday. But when I got back I realised that I just couldn't leave it like that. Faith never gave me the chance to explain about Michael. I needed to explain.' She sighed. 'The more I tried to track her down, the more I learnt about that world. I've spent the past six years hanging around the fringes, trying to keep track of Faith - I delved a little deeper and found out about you and Mel. That's when I decided that enough was enough.'

'So you decided to help people like me?' Natalie sounded angry, 'What is it you think you are saving us from?'

Claudia wasn't surprised by Natalie's reaction, 'I just believe in the freedom of choice,' she announced, 'I don't believe that people like Nash and Faith have the right to buy and sell slaves as they do.'

Natalie gave a tiny smile, 'The Freedom of choice … you sound like someone else.'

'Who?'

She waved her hand dismissively, it would take too long to explain about Leigh. 'So, you're on your own personal crusade?' she asked, the anger gone from her voice.

'I've never really thought about it like that,' Claudia replied, 'I just do what I feel is right.'

Natalie stared at her. There was so much more to it than that. Natalie was no psychotherapist but she knew people. Claudia's crusade wasn't just about doing the right thing - it was about making amends. Faith had tried to help Claudia and had got caught up in a dark chain of events. And when Faith had embraced that darkness, it had been Claudia's money that had made it possible. Claudia, as much as anyone, had helped to make Faith the woman she was. It was a harsh reality - but Natalie knew little else. She looked at Claudia and felt a deep empathy for her, 'Thank you.'

Claudia looked up, surprised.

'Thank you for telling me everything.'

She gave a tiny smile, 'It doesn't help though, does it? My life with Faith can not save you from her.'

'What can?' Natalie asked without really expecting an answer.

Claudia stared at her, she had no answer to give but she desperately wanted to find one. Eventually she said, 'You should go back to Mel.'

Natalie nodded slowly, 'I know.' She waited several long seconds before she slowly stood up. She managed

43

a tiny smile and then headed for the door. Claudia watched her go and then slowly sat back in her chair and closed her eyes as her mind swam with visions of Faith.

*

Claudia didn't go back to bed. She hadn't seen the point. If she managed to sleep then she knew that she would dream of Faith. It seemed better to sit through the last few hours of the night and choose the memories for herself.

It had been light for almost an hour when Mel entered the kitchen. She seemed surprised to see Claudia and offered a warm smile, 'Still up?'

Claudia managed a smile in response.

'Coffee?'

Claudia stared at the empty mug and nodded, 'Thanks.' She thought about what Mel had said in greeting, still up - it seemed likely that she knew that she had talked to Natalie, but how much had Natalie divulged?

'Are you okay?' Mel asked as she set two coffees down on the table.

Claudia managed a wan smile, 'Tired.'

'I'm not surprised. You and Natalie were talking for a good couple of hours.' A look flashed across Claudia's eyes that made Mel add, 'She didn't tell me anything and I don't need to know details - I can guess what you were talking about. Or rather, who.'

'Have you met her?'

'No,' Mel replied and remembered the card game that her Master had greatly enjoyed at his party weekend, 'But I've been on the receiving end of her ingenuity.'

Claudia stayed silent, waiting for Mel to explain further but it was clear that she wasn't going to elaborate.

'One thing about being the slave to a powerful Master

like Nash, he moved in powerful circles. I heard a lot about Faith, she's respected and feared in equal measure. And it's not just the slaves who fear her.'

Claudia nodded, 'Natalie told me that she came across a rival of Faith's in that slave-camp.' She paused, noticing the way that Mel's hands clenched into fists until the knuckles glowed white.

'I'm going to lose her, aren't I?' Mel asked suddenly, quietly.

'Is that what you want?'

'Of course it isn't!' Mel's voice was high with fear, 'I just don't know what I can do to stop it.'

'You know what Natalie needs … what you both need.'

Mel nodded, 'Of course. I don't want to hide from who we are but I can't be her Mistress and she can't be mine. But I'm so afraid that if we seek a release for our desires, we'll lose everything.'

'You don't have to, just remember - you're in control now.'

Mel shook her head, 'I don't mean than, I mean her … Faith. If we play on the edges, will she find us? I can't let Natalie live out her desires without fear of Faith taking her again - and if that happens, I'll never get her back.' She sighed with desperation, 'Faith marked Natalie and now she believes that she'll always own her. I wish I could scrape that scar from her skin, if I could then I'd make Faith forget about Natalie.'

Suddenly Claudia put her cup down and stood up.

'Where are you going?' Mel asked as Claudia headed for the door.

'I'm going to find an old friend and put and end to this once and for all.'

It took a moment for Mel to realise what she meant but by that time she was gone and Mel didn't know how to stop her.

Chapter 1.2:

The heavy atmosphere, thick with cigarette smoke, rolled out towards her as it had that first, fateful night when Michael had brought her here a lifetime ago. The club had hardly changed. The metal poles were still secured to the floor and ceiling. Hungry eyes watched the dancers from the shadows. But, where before a side door had led to a storeroom and offices, extensive building work had created a second club behind that door guarded by a heavy-set man. The back-room club had a select clientele but, after a week of visiting, the doorman recognised Claudia and stepped aside, giving her a small nod in greeting as she slipped a fifty pound note into his large palm. The door closed at her back, closing on the world behind her and, taking a deep breath, she once again stepped into the heavy atmosphere of the club beyond. If the club that she had passed through was thick with cigarette smoke, then this club was thick with sweat and lust. The smell of sex and desire was tangible, the sounds all too audible as gasps, groans and stifled screams echoed from the shadows. From the ceiling hung five cages - in four of the cages scantily dressed submissives, male and female, surveyed the action below. To Claudia's left, the remaining cage had been lowered on its winch to allow some men to play with the female submissive inside. As Claudia watched a thick bottle was slid between the bars and the submissive gasped as it disappeared between her thighs. The men laughed at her reaction, one of them flicking cigar ash at her naked breasts and making her cry out as tiny embers sprinkled her bare skin. Her cry deepened as the bottle was moved carefully, the contents - whatever they had been - dribbling between the slave's buttocks to puddle on the floor. A snapped order from one of the men and a male submissive quickly crawled over to lap the fluid from the floor. The male slave was wearing tight leather pants and as he bent forward to lap at the spilt alcohol, his exposed buttocks were revealed. The man with the cigar laughed again and found a new target for his cigar ash.

Claudia turned from the scene and found her eyes drawn to a female submissive pushed face-forward over one of the tables. The man who hammered her pussy had a firm grip on the handcuffs at her wrists, hauling her up and curving her back as he slammed into her. At her front, a Mistress nibbled and bit at one of the submissive's breasts while she ran a flickering candle flame over the other. The gagged submissive tossed her head from side to side, her eyes glazed and filled with tears. As Claudia walked past she couldn't help but notice the man's thick cock as he pulled free and spun her round. His cock glistened with juice and as he rammed back into the submissive she tossed her head as her body convulsed with pleasure. Claudia turned to the bar as the submissive's juices dribbled down the front of her thighs, gleaming in the twilight of the club's lighting.

Once she had got her drink she moved towards a table that she had discovered on her second visit. It was tucked away from the action at the main tables and afforded Claudia the opportunity to watch the club without being involved. However that hadn't stopped several leather or scantily clad men and women approaching the table with hope and interest glinting in their eager eyes. They had all been politely refused and Claudia had continued her vigil.

The blonde who approached the table that night was more reserved. Claudia watched her approach, studying the female lines beneath the black satin shirt and long leather skirt that was split to her hip on both legs. She was attractive and stirred something deep inside Claudia

47

- she almost regretted having to send her away.

'May I sit down?' the woman asked.

Claudia was about to refuse but instead found herself saying, 'If you like.'

The woman must have seen the reservation in Claudia's eyes because she half smiled, 'I've been watching you these past few days - I know that you don't participate. That's fine, I'm happy to talk.'

Claudia looked around, 'You want to talk?'

'Why not?' she sat down, close enough to hear Claudia but not so close to be invasive.

Claudia studied the woman with genuine interest, there was something strange about her, something that made her stand out but Claudia couldn't put her finger on what it was. She suddenly realised that she was staring and quickly rallied to answer the woman's question, 'You do know what sort of club this is, don't you?'

The woman gave a broad, genuine smile that was strangely infectious and Claudia smiled back.

Claudia sipped her drink, turning towards the door when some new arrivals appeared. She studied each one carefully before slowly lowering her gaze with a barely audible sigh.

'They're not there then?' the blonde asked.

'Who?' Claudia responded, setting her glass on the table.

'Whoever it is you're looking for.'

Claudia gave a small smile, 'You have been watching. Why?'

She gave a shrug, 'I was concerned - you look like you really don't want to be here.'

'It's hard,' Claudia announced, although she didn't know why she was suddenly talking to this stranger, 'So much has happened since I last saw her. I'm scared.'

'Scared of her, the past or the future?'

'All three,' Claudia sighed and picked up her drink, 'I'm sorry, you don't need to hear this.'

Before the blonde could answer a man suddenly appeared and Claudia recognised him as the doorman. 'Back room,' he announced quickly, 'Number four.' He didn't stop to see if she had heard or understood, just simply turned and left.

Claudia stared after him but didn't see him. Suddenly her mouth had gone dry and her heart was hammering in her chest.

'Are you okay?'

Claudia jumped at the question and half turned towards the blonde. 'What?'

'I asked if you were okay … you're shaking.'

Claudia stared at her hands as if seeing them for the first time - they were indeed shaking. She took a deep breath and then downed the rest of her drink. The blonde studied her in silence for several moments before apparently coming to a decision. She grabbed a napkin and then opened the small bag that she had been carrying. Removing an eyeliner pencil she scribbled something and slid it across the table. Claudia picked it up, out of courtesy more than anything, and studied the name and telephone number. 'Leigh Goldman.' she read out loud and the slid the napkin back, 'Thanks, but I don't need or want a date. Sorry.'

'I was offering you the chance to talk.'

Claudia half laughed, 'What are you? A psychotherapist?'

'Yes,' the blonde responded and stood up. 'Call me, I'd like to help if I can.'

Before Claudia could thank her, the blonde had moved back to the quiet corner from which she had emerged. Claudia noticed her beckon towards a dark-haired submissive before she was lost to the shadows. Claudia slipped the napkin into her pocket and then, taking a deep breath, she stood up and headed for the backrooms.

She found backroom number four and quietly opened the door. Once she had closed it behind her she stayed against the wall, hidden in the shadows. In the centre of the room was a circle of harsh, white light and a single figure. Claudia stared. Faith stood at the edge of the circle, the light just touching her. She stood with her arms crossed, waiting. Faith seemed to have grown in recent years, strengthened by her power. She wore her dominance like a cloak that seemed to electrify the room around her. She was as attractive as Claudia remembered - if not more so, her beauty increased by the sheer confidence and dominant power that made up her entire demeanour. She wore tight leather trousers and a black, silk shirt that accentuated her womanly, muscular curves. Just seeing her again was enough to make sweat bead on Claudia's upper lip and her pussy spasm, her breathing was ragged and her heart beat hard against her ribs.

Faith was not looking in Claudia's direction and seemed unaware of her. She seemed to be watching something happening on the far side of the circle of light. Claudia froze as there was a noise of footsteps approaching......

The naked submissive hit the floor hard and rolled into the circle of light. Her long blonde hair twisted around her neck and shoulders. Faith watched her impassively for several moments before she said, 'Kneel.' The command was simple and the submissive obeyed immediately, moving quickly to her knees, hands behind her back, head forward. She was young and pretty, slim and toned. Faith studied her in silence for an eternity before she eventually said, 'What do you want, slave?'

The submissive raised her head slightly but didn't look at Faith directly, 'I want to serve you, Mistress.'

Faith's laugh was curt, harsh and cruel, 'What makes you think that a pathetic whore like you could serve me?'

The submissive swallowed, clearly not knowing how to respond.

'Master Klein.' Faith said, half turning her head.

A man stepped from the shadows to stand beside Faith. He smiled at her and slowly took her hand in his, lifting it to his mouth and kissing the smooth flesh of the back of her hand. 'My beautiful Faith.'

She smiled back at him, 'Is this the slave that you were telling me about?'

He nodded, 'What do you think?'

'Tits are nice, arse is smooth - a little too smooth, her buttocks look almost virgin,' Faith responded. 'Have you beaten her?'

'A little light spanking from time to time but nothing else,' Klein responded.

'Did she like it?'

Klein shrugged and glanced at the submissive, 'Why don't you answer the Mistress, Hannah.'

'Master?' the submissive asked hesitantly.

'The Mistress would like to know if you enjoyed it when I spanked you. Why don't you tell her about the way your pussy juices up when I lay my hand across your buttocks.'

'Well?' Faith asked when the submissive was slow to answer.

'I like it … Mistress, when my Master spanks me.'

'Spanks,' Faith snarled, 'Pathetic. Those soft mounds deserve more than just a fucking spanking, don't you agree, slave?'

'I should be whipped, Mistress.'

'Too right you fucking should!' Faith yelled angrily. 'And who the fuck are you to tell anyone what should or shouldn't happen to that body? That is not your body,

51

you fucking whore, that is Master Klein's body, that is his tool to use and abuse as he wishes.' The young Mistress turned on him, 'Damn it, Klein, how dare you bring such an inexperienced, ill-disciplined slave into my club?'

'I will rectify the situation immediately,' Klein announced, 'On your fucking hands and knees!'

Hannah gave a small sob as she fell onto her hands, dipping her back to raise her buttocks - just as her Master had trained her.

'At least she has some training,' Faith sighed as she handed Klein a whip of leather strands, each at least three feet long and knotted at the ends. 'Lash her buttocks with that, let's see what the whore can take.'

Klein nodded and approached the submissive. 'Head up, slave, let us see your tears when they come.'

Hannah slowly raised her head, her blue eyes shining with fear and anticipation.

He laid the first lash across her buttocks and the sound of Hannah's gasp was loud in the otherwise silent room. He hit her again, increasing the strength of the blow and slicing her buttocks and upper thighs.

'Harder,' Faith ordered, her face impassive.

Klein lashed the submissive again, the strength of the blow drawing a cry from her lips. He lashed her over and over, her buttocks quivering beneath their first taste of the whip. Sweat stood out in beads along her spine that quivered as she was beaten.

'Let her pussy taste the whip.'

Hannah gave a cry at the sound of Faith's command and lifted her eyes to her Master, begging him with her tears not to do as Faith had asked. His lips curled into a snarl as he sliced the whip down across her reddened buttocks. 'Open your fucking legs!'

She sobbed as she slowly moved her thighs apart and

Klein grabbed her hips, hauling her up so that her legs were straight, her hands still on the floor.

'She's wet,' Faith announced, staring at Hannah's glistening cunt lips.

Klein nodded as he adjusted his position and raised the whip to shoulder height. He paused, allowing Hannah the time to fully anticipate the blow. When it fell she was silent for a moment before the shock faded and the full stinging burn seized her pussy. She screamed, falling back onto her knees, her hands pressed to her bruised lips.

Faith was furious, her arms uncrossed with a sudden sharp movement and she approached the slave with deliberate steps. She grabbed a handful of the submissive's hair and hauled her head up so that their faces were only inches apart. 'You want to serve me? You're pathetic!' She let go of Hannah's hair and grabbed her arms, flipping her onto her back. The submissive struggled but was no match for Faith's strength or clear experience and within moments her shoulders were pinned beneath Faith's knees, her face between the Mistress' thighs.

'Give me her ankles,' Faith ordered. Hannah kicked and struggled, crying out with fear but was silenced and subdued by Faith who reached down to grab her nipples and twist them harshly, saying, 'I will clamp these titties to the floor and have your Master fuck you into unconsciousness if you do not show the restraint befitting a whoreslave such as yourself.'

Hannah sobbed and fell silent as Klein grabbed her ankles and lifted her legs. Faith slipped her arms over the submissive's calves, pulling her legs up and taut, holding them firmly as Klein stood over the exposed and opened pussy. He raised the whip, once again allowing Hannah plenty of time to anticipate before the blow fell. Her scream was horrendous as the harsh leather sliced her cunt. The whip fell over and over, Klein increasing the strength of each blow as he delivered them.

'Oh God! Please! Stop!' Hannah cried, her only defence against the blows were her cries, her body was held immobile by Faith.

Klein paused in the beating and looked at Faith who stared back with cold eyes. 'A Master must have no pity for his slave. She is here to serve you. Her pussy, bruised as it is, is yours to do with as you wish. Beat her some more. Trust me, when you fuck her you will feel the difference.'

Klein nodded, licking his lips and raising the whip again. He beat her several more times before he suddenly cast the whip aside and quickly freed his hard, swollen cock from his trousers. He loomed over her red cunt and sank deep into her pussy, making her scream as he crushed her bruised lips. He fucked her harshly, his nails digging into her thighs. Suddenly he groaned and pulled back, his fist clenching around his cock and gripping it tightly as he sprayed his come over those tender, swollen lips. Once he was spent, he stumbled backwards, a smile playing at his lips.

Faith smiled back at him before she quickly reached forward and drove four fingers into the wide cunt. Hannah screamed loudly, her hips bucking up to meet the downward thrusts of the Mistress' fingers.

'You'd take my whole fucking hand right now,' Faith announced as she harshly finger-fucked the screaming slave, 'Would you like that? Would you like me to fist your cunt?' Faith gave a small laugh, 'Maybe Master Klein would like to fuck your arse while I slide my whole hand into your filthy pussy.'

The scream that erupted from Hannah's lips was piercing and her whole body quivered as she was racked by climax after climax until she fell limp and immobile.

There was silence for several moments and then Faith let go of Hannah's legs. The submissive groaned and rolled away, ending up near the edge of the light. Her glazed eyes stared into the shadows.

'Get out,' Faith ordered. 'You're pathetic.'

The sound of the Mistress' voice brought Hannah to her senses and she suddenly saw Claudia standing in the shadows. A flicker of surprise shone in her eyes and her mouth opened as if to ask a question.

'I said get out!' Faith snarled.

The submissive jolted as if she had been kicked and then quickly climbed to her feet. A glance from Faith and Klein gave a small nod before dragging his slave out of the room. He didn't seem to notice Claudia standing there and if he did then he showed no indication.

The door closed behind them and Claudia took a deep breath. She was about to step forward when she noticed Faith's shoulders tighten.

'I knew you were watching,' the young Mistress announced.

Claudia's heart that had been hammering against her ribs suddenly seemed to stop altogether.

Faith turned, glancing over her shoulder and fixing her stare on the shadows where Claudia was standing. The feel of those dark eyes boring into her set Claudia's heart racing once more. She walked slowly from the shadows and stood in the harsh white light while Faith studied her.

'You're looking good,' Faith announced.

'How did you know I was watching?'

'I know everything that goes on in this club,' Faith replied, there was anger in her voice as if she was annoyed that Claudia had underestimated her. 'Do you really think that you could spy on me in my world?'

There was no arrogance in the way that she said my world - just an honest truth that terrified Claudia. Claudia had been on the edge of this world for so many years, only recently had she delved so much deeper but now she was totally, and utterly, out of her depth. 'Don't look so scared,' Faith said and gave a smile that never reached her eyes.

Claudia considered denying her fear but realised that there was no point - Faith could still read her as easily as she ever could, even after all these years apart. Eventually Claudia said, 'We need to talk.'

'Ah, yes, let's talk,' Faith laughed, turning so that she could face Claudia. She looked so casual, so relaxed. Her actions only heightened how truly at home Faith was. 'Let's see, what shall we talk about? The weather? Politics? Or how about we talk about ... Natalie.' Anger had crept into her voice as she spoke.

Claudia tried to hold Faith's stare - it was difficult.

'I know it was you who stole her.'

'I didn't steal her - how could I steal something that was never yours to own?'

Faith's lips curled with amusement, 'Don't start the righteous freedom fighter bit, it's tiresome. I don't care if you believe she is my property or not. I do believe it and since you are in my world, my rules apply.'

'You know that I'm not just going to accept that.'

Faith shrugged, 'Your problem - not mine.'

Claudia was about to retaliate but stopped herself and took a deep breath. 'I always knew that I would see you again, someday, but I never wanted it to be like this.'

Faith's gaze softened, 'Me neither.'

'Then let's talk ... civilly ... we owe each other that at least.'

The young Mistress' eyes hardened again, 'I owe you nothing.'

'Don't say that - not after everything we went through.'

'I've been through worse.'

Claudia nodded, 'I suppose you have - I haven't'

'Not even with Peter Strick?' Faith asked, fixing her steely, blank gaze in place.

Claudia tensed at the memory that was still fresh and raw. 'You've been keeping track of me?'

'No. When Natalie went missing I traced her history and had a very interesting meeting with Peter Strick - he's an arrogant son-of-a-bitch, isn't he?'

Claudia stared at Faith. She didn't know what to say.

'Did you know that it was Natalie's mouth that you creamed over when Strick punished you and Mel?' Faith asked bluntly. The answer shone in Claudia's eyes. 'No?' she gave a small laugh. 'Well maybe you should thank her the next time you see her.'

Claudia managed to clear her throat, 'Who's to say that I'm going to see her?'

'Well, she is living in your rather nice studio flat, isn't she? I must say, it doesn't look as nice as our flat.'

Claudia went cold and her mouth abruptly dried. Fear settled in the pit of her stomach but not fear for herself - her fear was for Natalie and Mel. She turned to head for the door - she had to warn Natalie.

'The slave is safe … for now,' Faith announced, making Claudia stop and turn to face her, her eyes suspicious.

Claudia studied the young Mistress and then the light of realisation slowly spread over her features. 'You knew that I would come and find you.'

Faith nodded slowly.

A part of Claudia was flattered and warmed by her admission - it was nice to think that Faith had been expecting her. But then she remembered how many years had passed and what those years had done to the young woman before her. She recalled her conversation with

Natalie, she had advised the ex-slave to see Faith as two different people and now she needed to take her own advice. It was perhaps made a little easier by the scene that had played out before her eyes just a short time ago.

'I've never forgotten you,' Faith announced suddenly, 'I guess it's thanks to you that I'm where I am today.'

Claudia's voice dripped anger as she replied, 'Well, I'm just glad that my money could open the door for you.'

'I didn't mean that,' Faith responded, a strange tone to her voice. She didn't explain further and paused just long enough to bring her emotional shutters down once more. 'So, is that the reason for your little crusade? You're trying to make amends for letting me loose on the world?'

'Something like that.'

'Well, don't bother,' Faith snarled, 'I don't want anyone making apologies for me.'

'Then what do you want?'

'The same thing as you,' Faith responded simply.

Claudia frowned - not understanding.

'You came here to try and talk me round to your way of thinking. You somehow want me to see things the way you do.'

Claudia stared at her, her face expressionless.

'Well, I just want the same opportunity. You've taken on this crusade to save poor, defenceless slaves and that's all very noble. So I'll give you the opportunity to explain your side further but I want the chance to do the same.'

'I don't understand.'

'Spend the weekend with me.'

'What?'

'I'm calling a ...' she paused and allowed a small smile to creep over her lips, '... a summit meeting. I'm offering us both the opportunity to put our points across. I believe you were the one who said we owe each other.'

Claudia shook her head, 'I'm not going anywhere with you.'

'You don't trust me?'

'No.'

Faith stared at her, 'Then why did you come here?'

'What?'

'You found me - remember? I want to know why.'

'Because I loved you.'

Faith paused, a strange look flashed across her eyes, 'Loved - as in, did love?'

Claudia couldn't answer and they locked stares.

'Spend the weekend with me,' Faith announced, breaking the stare, 'You have my word that you will be able to leave at anytime and … you will have my word that I'll forget all about Natalie.'

'What?' Claudia was stunned.

'Spend the weekend with me and I'll forget Natalie.'

*

'You're joking.'

Claudia shook her head, carefully studying Mel through a haze of cigarette smoke.

Mel ran a hand through her raven hair. She glanced over her shoulder, as if searching for Natalie. They could both still hear the shower so Claudia continued, 'I have to do it.'

Mel wanted to argue, to say something that would somehow change everything but how many times had she wished that with equal futility?

'I'm not just doing it for Natalie's sake,' Claudia announced as if that would somehow make everything better. 'There's so much between Faith and me -'

'Was.' Mel corrected. She had learnt more about Claudia and Faith in the past week. 'You've said it yourself - she's not the person you knew.'

'I have to be sure of that.'

'Do you?' Mel was aghast and angry. 'That woman burned her initial in Natalie's flesh - were you in love with someone capable of doing that, and worse?'

'Are you trying to talk me out of spending the weekend with her?' Claudia asked, not unkindly. 'This is your best chance of getting Natalie away from her.'

'I know,' Mel sighed, 'But I won't save Natalie at any cost. There must be limits.'

Claudia nodded, 'I appreciate that.' The sound of the shower being turned off made her stop. She leant forward across the table. 'She isn't to know,' Claudia hissed, meaning Natalie. Mel nodded her agreement but it was clear that she didn't like any of this but there was nothing that she could do.

Chapter 1.3:

Even though the inner club had no windows, it still looked incredibly different in the daytime. The smoke may have been cloying at night, the lights dimmed and providing a seedy atmosphere but it was preferable to the harsh, tacky feel of the club during the day. The lights were too bright, the air stale and the entire inner club was altogether too empty. Faith was sitting at the bar, sipping from a tumbler that clinked ice. She set the glass on the bar and directed for the barman to pour her another drink. As he shook a small bottle of orange juice, Faith lit herself a cigarette and slipped the lighter into her pocket. When the barman had poured her drink she gave a slight nod and the barman disappeared into the storeroom behind the bar, closing the door. Faith inhaled a lungful of smoke and exhaled slowly before saying out loud, 'Are you going to stand there all day?'

Claudia took a deep breath and slowly approached the bar.

'Do you want a drink?'

'No, thank you.'

Faith glanced at her, 'Hungry?'

Claudia shook her head. She hadn't eaten breakfast or lunch, she hadn't been able to face food of any sort. She regretted that now as her lips quivered and her stomach grumbled.

Faith gave a tiny smile, 'Sure? We've got a long drive ahead.'

'Where are we going?'

'To my house in the country.'

Claudia allowed herself a smirk, 'You have a house in the country?'

'Among others, yeah.'

'How many houses do you have?'

'Enough.' she smiled, 'I've come a long way since we first met - back then I didn't have anywhere to live. Now I've got homes in six countries.'

'I didn't know that … about you being homeless when we first met.'

Faith's eyes grew distant, 'I used to sleep here, at the club. The manager made me sleep under his desk.'

Claudia was stunned, 'Why did you never tell me that?'

'Because I don't want your damn pity - I never wanted that!' Faith was suddenly angry and Claudia took a step backwards as the dark shutters came down over Faith's eyes, 'I am what I am. If I'm a product of my past, who gives a shit? Unlike you and all the little helpless slaves, I don't feel the need to question myself constantly - I learnt to accept what I am a long time ago.'

And that was it - that was what made Faith stand out from every other Mistress and Master, that was why she was so at home in this world, simply because she just accepted her place within it. Claudia stared at Faith and for the briefest of moments she actually envied the Mistress and the freedom that her acceptance brought. The emotion passed just as quickly when Claudia considered the cost to Natalie of Faith's indulgence in her freedom.

'Ready?' Faith asked, tossing back the last of her drink and dropping the cigarette butt into the glass.

Claudia nodded dumbly - not trusting her voice.

'All right then.' Faith hopped off the stool and led the way.

Outside the club Faith led Claudia to a sleek black car. It looked expensive and powerful but Claudia didn't even attempt to identify the make or model. Faith climbed into the back seat, closing the door behind her and obviously expecting Claudia to go round the other side. She did so, trying desperately to steady her breathing as she went. Opening the door, she climbed into the back and glanced at Faith. The young Mistress smiled but it never reached her eyes. Turning to the front, Faith said, 'Let's go.'

Claudia looked at the driver, catching his profile as he started the engine. He was vaguely handsome, his mouth was set in a harsh, line. Perhaps feeling Claudia's eyes on him, he shifted so that he could look at her in the rear-view mirror. After he had studied her, he released the handbrake and pulled away from the kerb.

The driver never turned or spoke during the journey and Faith didn't engage in conversation either. From time to time Faith would make a call on her mobile and speak cryptically. Claudia was grateful that she couldn't understand what she was saying, she had the feeling that she didn't really want to know. Eventually, with Faith's ambiguous words floating around the car, Claudia drifted off to sleep.

She awoke with a start, grabbing at the back of the seat in front. The driver half glanced at her as he pulled on the handbrake. Once he had cut the engine he climbed from the vehicle, closing the door behind him. Claudia looked around, they were parked in a lay-by on a narrow lane with trees either side. 'Where are we?' she asked Faith who was reaching for the door handle.

'I've got some business to attend to,' Faith announced and climbed out of the car, 'Come with us if you want.'

Claudia climbed out of the car, surprised to see the driver standing by the boot. When she saw Faith approach him, she followed.

'Open it.' Faith instructed the driver. With a curt nod, he lifted the lid of the boot and Claudia felt a gasp tear from her throat. Curled on her side in the boot, naked and filthy, was Hannah. Her hands were bound behind her back, her ankles bound similarly. A cloth blindfold had been tied around her eyes and was wet with tears. She hadn't been gagged and her breath came in short, fearful gasps.

'What the fuck is this?' Claudia demanded.

'This is not your concern. Come with us or stay in the car, your choice, but do not interfere.' Faith responded calmly as she waved at the driver to remove the submissive from the boot.

'Can I ask what you are doing with her?'

'Her Master asked me to take her for a while and show her some discipline. She's a worthless whore who needs to be taught some lessons in how to behave. Her Master is up and coming, he wants a slave befitting his new status. If I can not correct this whore's behaviour, he will be obliged to replace her.' Faith grabbed Hannah's chin, lifting her head and Claudia realised that the little speech hadn't really been meant for her. 'The whore has had a far too easy time of it, I am going to teach her what it really means to be a slave … no more games.' Hannah gave a small whimper as Faith tightened her grip on her jaw before letting go. 'Bring her,' Faith snarled and then headed off towards the trees. Claudia followed her as the driver picked Hannah up and put her over his shoulder as if she weighed nothing.

Faith followed a path through the trees that led to a hedge and a field beyond that slopped upwards, cutting any view of the horizon. The path ended at a wooden stile. 'Put her on here,' Faith ordered.

Nodding, the driver carried Hannah forward and climbed onto the step of the stile. Lifting her from his shoulder, he positioned her with her thighs either side of the top plank. She cried out as her pussy was crushed against the rough wood and with her wrists and ankles still bound it was hard to keep her balance. The driver reached down and expertly loosened the length of rope that joined her ankles so that her feet could drop either side of the plank she sat on and rest on the stepping plank.Hannah's ankles rested securely but still she wobbled dangerously. The driver needed no instruction and quickly looped a length of rope around the bonds at her wrists. Pulling the rope back, he tied it to the post, forcing the slave to arch her back and thrust her chest forwards. Once the rope was secure he slipped a further length around her thighs and calves to secure her to the stile. Claudia had been so fascinated by the driver's bondage expertise that she hadn't notice Faith disappear into the woods. She only noticed when the Mistress returned, carrying a length of bramble in a gloved hand and a thin sapling in the other.

'Take her blindfold off,' Faith announced. 'I want her to see this.'

The driver did as he was asked and then jumped down from the stile.

Hannah squinted against the sudden glare, tears rolling down her cheeks. When she saw Faith, her eyes filled with real fear at the sight of the bramble and makeshift whip. 'What shall we start with?' Faith asked, lifting both hands as if weighing the two objects. She clearly didn't expect anyone to answer and she continued to ask herself over and over before she eventually slipped the sapling under her arm and handed the glove and length of bramble to the driver.

He took it and slipped the glove on, wrapping the end of the bramble around his thick fist. 'Where?' he asked, his voice heavy with anticipation.

'Umm … the breasts I think,' Faith replied, her response bringing a whimper from Hannah.

'How many?'

Faith studied the bound submissive, tipping her head to the side, 'How many would a whore like you be able

65

to take?' she smiled cruelly. 'Let's find out. Whip her until she begs you to stop.'

The driver nodded and approached the slave as Faith and Claudia stepped back. He straightened the length of bramble and then brought it swinging towards the submissive's prominent breasts. The tiny barbs dug into the sensitive flesh and Hannah cried out, turning her head from the blow. The driver yanked the bramble back, making sure that the barbs tore free of her flesh and making her cry out again. Tiny beads of blood quickly appeared on both breasts. He hit her again, catching her just above her nipples and making the hard buds quiver as he pulled the bramble free. He beat her for several minutes before the sobbing slave suddenly screamed out loud as the bramble tore at her quivering and vulnerable breasts.

'Oh God, please, Mistress, make him stop!'

Faith sighed angrily, 'Pathetic. Absolutely, fucking pathetic.' She handed the driver the thin sapling, 'Ten blows across the breasts, let's really make her cry.'

Hannah was already sobbing uncontrollably and when the sapling whipped down across her already wounded breasts, her cry was horrendously loud and pitiful. She took the next nine blows with a similar response, tossing her head from side to side and screaming loudly. Once the final blow had landed, Faith waved for the driver to untie her. Once she was free, he lifted her from the stile and threw her onto the ground where she lay sobbing, wrists and ankles still bound. Faith moved towards the stile, studying the upper plank. 'Look at that wetness there,' she gave a small laugh. 'Our little whore enjoyed that.'

The driver laughed, licking his lips.

'I love the way the wood gets dark where a slave creams on it,' Faith stared into the distance. 'The pole that Natalie was wrapped around had a dark stain on it after I had branded her.' She turned and approached Hannah, 'How about I give you a nice brand, eh?'

Hannah shivered uncontrollably as Faith approached.

'I could burn my letter into your arse or maybe your breast. Would you like that?'

Hannah shook her head, 'No, Mistress,' she sobbed.

Faith's lip curled with fury and she bent to snatch a handful of Hannah's hair, yanking her head up, 'What did you say?'

'Mistress?'

'I asked what you said.'

Hannah swallowed as best she could, 'I said …' she couldn't finish the sentence.

'Did you dare to refuse me?'

'No, Mistress.'

'And now you are lying … my God, is there no end to your indiscipline?' Faith yelled. She grabbed Hannah by the arms and hauled her up, dragging her back to the stile and throwing her half over it. Hannah cried out as she tried to support herself. Faith released her ankles, allowing her feet to support some of her weight while her upper body hung over the stile. Faith ran her hand over the smooth buttocks that had healed from her previous attentions. She looked up at the driver and nodded at the whip-like sapling. 'Please beat some discipline into this whore.'

'With pleasure,' the man announced.

'Keep count, whore,' Faith ordered. 'That is the first sign of a disciplined slave, one who can count their punishment without error.'

Hannah sobbed, her hands clenching into fists behind her back. The switch landed across the centre of her twin mounds, pushing into the flesh and making the mounds swell around it. Hannah screamed, 'One!' Another blow and then another fell onto her quivering buttocks and the numbers tore from her throat. 'Five! ... Six! ... Seven! ...' The blows came steadily, the driver allowing her buttocks the time to settle so that he could aim the next blow carefully. He delivered a series of blows to her upper thighs, slicing the whip upwards so that it hit just below the swell of her buttocks and making the submissive stand on her toes. She almost tipped over the stile but a well-aimed blow to the top of her buttocks dragged her down again. 'Fifteen!' Hannah screamed and sobbed. Faith raised her hand, 'That will do.'

Nodding the driver stepped back as Faith approached the slave again. 'Now I'll ask you again. Should I burn my letter into your flesh?'

Hannah swallowed painfully, 'Yes, Mistress, if it would please you.'

Faith nodded and then turned to the driver, 'Now fuck this whore and then we can get on.'

Hannah's head shot up and she looked over her shoulder to see the driver climb onto the stile, his thick penis already out of his trousers. He positioned at her entrance but didn't move. He seemed to be waiting for an instruction from Faith. The Mistress studied Hannah carefully and was particularly interested in the ripples of anticipation that ran up and down her spine.

'How close are you to coming, John?' Faith asked the driver.

He smiled, 'Pretty close. That beating really got me going.'

'Fuck her quickly then and let's see how much she enjoyed that thrashing.'

Smiling broadly, the driver sank his thick cock into Hannah's slick cunt. The submissive gasped, hanging her head. Faith grabbed a handful of the slave's hair and dragged it up so that she could examine every emotion the slave went through while she was fucked.

'A slave should never be allowed a hiding place. She must learn to display how much she enjoys her beatings.' Faith glanced along Hannah's body to where the driver stood between the flogged buttocks, his cock inside her and waiting to deliver Hannah's next lesson.

'Fuck her, John,' Faith said pleasantly and continued to hold the slave's face up for examination.

John gripped the slave's hips and pulled free before driving back in, this time making her scream. He fucked her fast, drilling into her wide pussy and rocking the stile with the force of his thrusts. After a few minutes a soft whine started in Hannah's throat. The whine grew until it became a cry and then finally a scream as her whole body tensed and then relaxed. The driver fucked her limp body for a few more moments before, with a growl, her climaxed deep in her sopping cunt.

*

It was getting dark when they arrived at the large country house and Claudia couldn't help but be impressed with the size of the property and grounds. But then she remembered how Faith had been able to finance it all and she felt a cold stone in the pit of her stomach - after all, it had been her money that had set Faith on her path. She pushed that thought to the back of her mind as the car slowed to a halt and they climbed out. Faith led Claudia into the house while the driver went round to the back of the car, to let the slave out Claudia assumed.

They entered the large hallway and Claudia looked round as they crossed the carpeted floor. 'I'll give you the tour tomorrow … maybe,' Faith announced without any real conviction and then led Claudia to the stairs. 'You'll sleep in the room next to mine.' she told her and half smiled when she saw the look of relief on Claudia's face, 'Did you think I was going to put you in my room?'

Claudia shrugged, the thought had crossed her mind but she'd be damned if she'd let Faith know that.

'You come to me when you're ready,' Faith said with more conviction than when she had offered the tour.

Claudia wasn't sure what she expected to see when Faith opened the door to her own bedroom, she hadn't been in the bedrooms of many Mistresses. She perhaps wouldn't have been surprised to see chains hanging from black walls, or whips hanging from hooks. She certainly didn't expect to see a lithe, tanned, beautiful and above all - naked - young woman. The young woman fell to her knees as Faith entered, straight, very long, black hair falling like a curtain around her face.

'This is Max,' Faith announced, waving at the young slave as if introducing the family pet.

Claudia scanned the tastefully decorated room, the action preferable to looking at the kneeling slave. Her eyes came to rest on a small, thin mattress on the floor at the end of the large four-poster bed.

'You're sleeping with John until further notice,' Faith told the slave. 'Take your bed with you.'

Max's head shot up, 'Mistress?'

Faith rounded on her, the slave shrinking under her harsh stare. 'See that he gives you thirty lashes for questioning me, you fucking whore!'

Claudia was stunned by Faith's sudden fury and cruelty.

'Yes, Mistress,' Max whispered, 'I'm sorry, Mistress.'

'Get the fuck out of my sight!'

'Yes, Mistress,' she jumped to her feet and quickly rolled up the thin mattress. Faith turned her back on the slave and approached the antique dressing table. With her Mistress' back turned, Max paused on her way to the door and stared at Claudia. Claudia felt a cold chill run down her spine as the slave stared at her with a look of sheer hate. Claudia wanted to say something, to tell her that she had no intention of usurping the slave but she doubted that the young woman would hear a word.

'Is that whore still fucking here?' Faith asked without turning around.

The fury and hate in Max's eyes turned abruptly to fear before she hurried out of the room.

Claudia took a deep breath once the door had closed. 'Is my room next door?'

'Next door down the hall,' Faith replied, 'It's en-suite and should have everything you need.' The Mistress turned slowly, 'Unless you want to stay here.'

'And what would your slave think of that?'

A confused look flashed across Faith's face as if Claudia was speaking a different language. In the end she gave a small shrug, 'I'm here if you change your mind.'

'I won't,' Claudia replied as she headed for the door.

'Someone will bring you some food.'

'Thank you,' Claudia replied automatically and then hurried out.

The room was just as tastefully decorated if not as expensive. The bag that Claudia had brought had been placed on the bed. She grabbed the bag and opened it, deciding to try and keep busy for the time being. She moved the bag to the chest of drawers and pulled the top drawer open. Her hand froze on the drawer as she stared at the contents. The draw was filled with sex-toys. Vibrators, dildos, butt-plugs, handcuffs, whips and several other items that Claudia couldn't even identify. She managed to close her eyes and slowly slid the drawer shut, trying to swallow past the dryness of her mouth.

She had unpacked the bag and was just thinking about having a bath when there was a soft knock at the door.

She went to it and pulled it open. A middle-aged man gave a curt nod, 'The Mistress asked if I could bring you something to eat. What would you like, madam?'

Claudia wanted to laugh but her stomach rumbled. 'What's on offer?'

'Whatever you wish, madam. We have a well-stocked kitchen.'

She thought for a moment, 'I'd kill for a chicken, salad sandwich.'

The man stared at her, a slight twitch jumping in his cheek. 'A chicken, salad sandwich?'

'Please. With chips?'

'Chips.'

'If you don't mind.'

'Of course.'

'Thank you.'

The man turned and Claudia closed the door. Sniggering to herself, she went to find the bathroom.

The bath relaxed her perfectly and she ate her food while lying on the bed. When she was finished she stretched and yawned and then slowly her eyes drifted to the chest of drawers and in particular the top drawer. She remembered Hannah and what the driver, John, had done to her. She particularly remembered Hannah's shuddering climax as he had violently fucked her and felt her own pussy begin to ache. She stood up and walked slowly towards the chest of drawers.

CHAPTER 1.4:

Breakfast was, thankfully, not as lavish as Claudia had feared it would be. Faith had met her at her room and, after asking how she had slept, had shown her downstairs to a medium-sized, bright room with a large round table and four chairs. Only two places had been set and Claudia didn't know whether to be relieved or apprehensive that it was to be just her and Faith eating. In the end, as with everything else, she would just have to go with the flow. The table had been placed in front of a set of double doors that let in the fresh smell of the country, bright spring sunshine glinted off the dewy grass and Claudia hadn't realised how much she had missed the simple peace to be found away from the city. She turned to say as much to Faith, determined to bring a quality of normality to her breakfast, but as she looked at the younger woman she couldn't help but stare. The sun glinted off her brown locks and lighted her face, showing her wonderful profile as she looked towards the door. Claudia wanted to tear her eyes away but she couldn't - she could only stare as Faith turned back to her and mouthed silent words. Claudia shook her head, regaining her senses. 'I'm sorry?'

A smile creased Faith's lips, 'I asked if you wanted a coffee.'

'Oh ... yes, please.'

Faith nodded to her right and Claudia looked up to see the naked slave, Max, standing beside Faith, holding a silver coffee pot. As the slave poured the coffee into her Mistress' cup, Faith asked, 'Why were you staring?'

'Hmm?' Claudia asked innocently, causing Faith to smile.

'You were staring at me ... I was wondering why?'

Claudia considered lying but what was the point? She

had come here this weekend to try and convince Faith to see certain truths but what would be the point if she didn't face them herself? 'I realised that you were still beautiful,' Claudia announced.

Max moved so that she could pour coffee into Claudia's cup.

'Does that mean that you still love me?' Faith asked, a slight hesitancy in her voice as if she were afraid of the answer.

Before Claudia could answer she suddenly gasped and leapt to her feet as a stream of hot coffee was poured into her lap. Claudia swiped at the coffee with her napkin, managing to wipe most of it away before it could burn her. Sighing with relief, Claudia looked up at Max and found the slave staring at her with the same look of sheer hatred that she had shown the previous night as she slowly righted the pot.

'What the fuck are you doing?' Faith demanded.

Max didn't look at her Mistress or even respond. She just stared at Claudia with that hate filled stare - it was as if, at that moment in time, nothing else existed but the two of them and her hate.

'John! Get in here!' Faith bellowed, snatching the coffee pot from Max's hands and surely burning her palm on it as she slammed it down on the table - but her own fury was such that she didn't even notice.

The door opened and the driver walked quickly to the table. 'Mistress?' he queried.

Claudia glanced at him - he wasn't a male-slave but he still treated Faith with the utmost respect. It was quickly becoming clear that Faith's reputation as one of the most well-known and respected Mistresses in the country was well deserved.

'Look what this stupid whore has done!' Faith unleashed her anger on John, making him flinch as if her words had struck him. She directed a gesture towards Claudia who started to say that it didn't matter but Faith waved her into silence.

'I'll deal with it right away.'

Nodding angrily, Faith sat back down as John dragged the slave towards the open double doors. 'Bring us another pot of coffee,' Faith said loudly, clearly expecting someone to hear her.

Claudia turned and watched as John pushed Max onto the long, stone veranda that stretched along the outside wall of the house. The veranda widened in stages, the section outside the door was the most narrow which meant that Claudia had a clear view as John forced the slave to bend forward and grab the ornate concrete parapet along the outside edge of the veranda. He slipped a thin crop from his belt and rested it against the slave's buttocks. Then, taking a breath, he raised the crop and brought it slicing down across the firm mounds. The retort was loud and made Claudia jump as she quickly looked away. She sat back down at the table and laid the damp napkin beside her plate, fiddling with the edging. The sound of the punishment continued and on the edge of her peripheral vision, Claudia could see John raising his arm over and over again. Faith watched the punishment until the door opened and a young girl, dressed in jeans and a tight t-shirt, brought a fresh pot of coffee.

'Shall I wait and serve you, Mistress?' she asked, keeping her head bowed.

Faith shook her head and waved her away before pouring Claudia a cup. Claudia was grateful to have something to do and she quickly added sugar and milk, trying to ignore the sound of the beating as she stirred her drink.

The thrashing continued for several minutes until the

constant beat of the crop striking the slave's flesh was mirrored in a dull throb at Claudia's temple. She rubbed her fingers in a circle at the side of her eyebrow and let out a sigh, prompting Faith to ask what was wrong. Claudia glanced at the veranda. The slave's buttocks rippled under another blow and the reddened flesh glistened with sweat. 'Don't you think she's had enough?'

Faith frowned, yet again her face held that look of incomprehension before Claudia's words finally found their target. The young mistress sighed and waved her hand at John. 'That will do, continue as you wish.'

John nodded and laid the crop on the parapet before grabbing the slave's shoulder, turning her round and forcing her to her knees. 'Breakfast for you, slut.' he laughed and unfastened his trousers. The sound of the slave deep-throating John did little to help Claudia's appetite but it was preferable to the sound of her being beaten.

'So, what have you been up to?'

Claudia stared at Faith. The question was so normal and spoken so easily that it caught her completely off guard. A slave with welt lined buttocks was just a few feet away, her head bobbing as she was forced to swallow an engorged penis, and Faith could have just as casually asked her about the weather.

'I assume you've been doing more than just keeping tabs on me,' Faith added when Claudia didn't respond.

'I … um …' Claudia cleared her throat, '… I do a bit of freelance work from time to time.'

'Just earning pocket money though, eh? I assume mummy and daddy still look out for you?'

'I have an allowance but we've hardly spoken since …' she let the sentence trail off.

Faith didn't seem keen to continue that line and so she

asked, 'What sort of freelance work?'

'Art consultancy.'

Faith smiled, 'You and your art appreciation. Do you remember that exhibition that you took me to? The Tate wasn't it?'

'Yes, the Tate Modern,' Claudia replied with a nod and couldn't help but smile. An exhibition of post-modern art, which had failed to impress the young, streetwise Faith. She remembered how awkward and out of place Faith had looked and now she was feeling that herself. Claudia looked up at Faith and found the young woman staring at her. Her lips were curled into the tiniest of smiles, an expression that Claudia hadn't seen for so long. For the briefest of moments she could almost forget the past six years and allow herself the luxury of drowning in Faith's dark eyes - as she had so often before. Faith blinked, slowly and deliberately, breaking the moment. Claudia sat back, realising that Faith had intentionally broken eye contact.

'You spend too much time in the past,' Faith announced.

'You can still read me as well as ever,' Claudia replied.

'But do you see what I mean?' Faith sighed. 'I can read you because I'm good at reading people's expressions. It's a skill that I've developed and put to good use. I don't need the past to help so why drag it up?'

Claudia fought down the urge to respond with because it's all I have but knew that it would sound childish. Instead she settled for, 'Why do you seem so intent on forgetting the past? Were you that intent about forgetting me?'

Faith shook her head, 'I never forgot you.'

'Watch the teeth, slut,' John hissed.

The two women turned their attention back to the scene

77

on the veranda. The lithe, black haired girl was still kneeling before the man, holding herself steady by gently clasping his buttocks while she rode his thrusts into her face; using the softness of her mouth to service the man who had so savagely punished her just a few minutes before.

Faith frowned and stared at her slave with an expression close to amusement. Before Claudia could continue their conversation, Faith asked, 'Have you had enough to eat?'

Claudia hadn't eaten a thing but she nodded anyway, reaching for her coffee and downing the last dregs from the cup. To her right John suddenly groaned and bucked his hips. Turning quickly away, Claudia stood up and followed Faith.

Once back in her room, Claudia stripped and showered, washing away the wetness that had collected between her thighs - it wasn't just coffee. She tried to force the sounds of the slave being beaten from her mind and found herself thinking of Natalie. She reminded herself of what Faith had done to the unfortunate slave and that helped to calm her and stop the urge to retrieve something from the top drawer. Turning the shower temperature to nearly freezing, she forced herself to stay under the jet for several moments, gasping as the cold took her breath away. Eventually she turned the water off and climbed from the shower.

When she was dressed, Claudia went to Faith's room, deciding that it was time to discuss their different ideals. She knocked on the door and then opened it when Faith called out. The young Mistress had also showered, her hair glistened darkly around her shoulders, the weight of the water straightening the loose curls. Claudia had always loved it when Faith was fresh out of the shower - loved it so much in fact that on many occasions she had taken Faith back in to the shower to enjoy some intimate time together beneath the spray. Claudia shook her head as if to dislodge the past from her mind.

'No permanent damage from the coffee, I hope,' Faith said, sitting on the bed and lighting a cigarette. She tossed the packet to Claudia who took one and lit it before replying, 'It didn't soak through, I'm fine.

'That's good. I don't know what got into the stupid whore. She's not normally that clumsy.'

Claudia exhaled smoke, 'She doesn't like me.'

'What?' there was humour in Faith's voice.

'I don't think your slave likes me.'

Faith laughed, 'She probably sees you as a threat. Her loyalty is to me. She would die for me without question or hesitation.'

'I didn't realise that you were able to command such emotions in others,' Claudia said even as she tried to ignore the part of her mind that reminded her that she would have done the same once.

'Oh, it's not a natural emotion - I made her that way,' Faith announced matter-of-factly. 'I was going to make Natalie the same way, that's why I sent her to that camp.' Claudia stared at her, eyes wide and disbelieving. Never before had Faith seemed so far removed from the young woman that Claudia had loved. Faith didn't seem to notice Claudia's reaction as she continued, 'Did you see Max when she was being punished this morning? She never flinched, did she? Never cried out?' the mistress smiled. 'It took a long time to make her that way.'

Claudia didn't really want to know what Faith meant. There had been a tone to Faith's voice that had chilled Claudia to her very core. She didn't want to know Max's history, she didn't want to know what Faith had done to the slave. But somehow she heard herself ask, 'What did you do?'

79

Faith stared up at her, perhaps surprised that Claudia had asked further. She drew on the cigarette, the smoke escaping a moment later through her smile-curved lips. 'I very much doubt that you will ever have the opportunity to meet a slave like Max ever again. She really is quite something. A keen submissive, I hired her as a dancer and a slave at my club. I saw her strength immediately and in her I saw the opportunity to explore an idea that I had considered for some time. You see, Max is my silent slave.'

Claudia frowned.

'In matters of pleasure and pain - Max will not make a sound,' Faith explained.

Claudia wasn't sure that she believed her but she still asked, 'You trained her to do that?'

Faith nodded, 'Her training, although torturous, was quite simple. I had her fucked regularly in a variety of ways. But anytime she made a sound, the fucking stopped immediately and cold water was poured onto her breasts and pussy. Then, half an hour or maybe an hour later, we would begin again. It continued like that for three days and nights - we allowed her no sleep - which didn't matter because she was too aroused to sleep anyway.' Faith paused to stub out her cigarette. She looked at Claudia as she continued, 'Have you ever been left on the point of climax, over and over again? It causes terrible cramps in the abdomen. By the middle of the second day we had to give her muscle relaxants to ease the terrible cramping when we realised that her cries were from more than just arousal. And then we continued again. It was near the end of the third day when she finally climaxed. It was incredible - her whole body shook and her pussy seemed to explode in a shower of juice - but not a sound escaped her lips. It was exquisite.

'That was only the start. Things continued in a similar

way and I had her pleasured in a variety of ways ...'
Faith sighed wistfully, 'My God, the things we did to
her and the tools we used. There was this one vibrator -
I had it especially made - we could control everything
about it, speed, length, girth, with a slight adjustment I
could even make it bend the way I wanted.'

Claudia was saved from further reminiscing by a knock
at the door. Faith stood and went to open it and there, as
if on cue, was Max. The slave was naked, her skin shining
with a film of sweat. Once again Claudia couldn't help
but marvel at the slave's beauty.

'Once I had trained her to take pleasure without making
a sound - then it was time to do the same with pain.'
Faith explained as she led Max to stand in front of
Claudia. 'We started with the whip. If she could take ten
blows without crying out then she was pleasured. As
long as she made no sound during her pleasure then we
would allow her to climax. If she made a sound while
being pleasured, we would stop and apply the cold water.
Then we would start the whipping again. It only took a
day before she took ten lashes and the pleasure without
making a sound. Her entire training took a year. Various
pleasures and tortures were devised and she learned to
silently take them all. When she was finished, I gave her
this ...' Faith turned Max so that Claudia could see her
buttocks. She had no idea why she hadn't seen it the
night before but there was a perfect F burned into her
flesh. '... she didn't make a sound.' Faith finished.

Claudia stared at the young Mistress - she knew that
there was disbelief in her eyes but she couldn't help it.
Claudia had seen a lot in the past few years and had
been on the receiving end of enough. She just couldn't
bring herself to accept what Faith was saying. How could
anyone really suffer the branding of their flesh without
making a sound?

'You don't believe me?' Faith asked, there was anger in her voice that surprised Claudia. That surprise remained until Claudia realised that her very disbelief was a challenge to Faith's power. She hadn't meant it as such but it was too late to take it back - but she had to try. 'It's not that I don't believe you,' Claudia began, her mind racing to find the words that would calm the angry fires in Faith's eyes, 'It's just that -'

Faith never let her finish. 'A demonstration then!'

'Faith, I -'

'Sit down over there,' Faith ordered, waving at a chair in the corner of the room.

'Faith, please.'

'I said sit over there.' There was a dark anger in Faith's eyes that sent Claudia to the chair.

There was no point in arguing further so Claudia moved to the chair and sat down, wishing that she could somehow avoid the demonstration that Faith was about to give. But there was no escape. All she could do was sit and watch.

Faith moved to the door and pulled it open. She called for John and then moved back into the room to sit on the edge of the bed. John entered a few moments later and looked questioningly at Faith.

'Close the door.'

He did so, his glance moving from Faith to Max, to Claudia and then back to Faith. 'Mistress?'

Faith leant back a little, 'I want you to show my friend how to treat a slave.'

John's eyes widened with delight, 'With pleasure.' He fixed his gaze on Max and licked his lips.

'Good,' Faith picked up the cigarettes and lighter and tossed them onto the end of the bed, 'Start with those.'

Smiling, John picked up the cigarettes and lit himself one, puffing the smoke into Max's face. 'On your knees,' he ordered.

Max dropped to her knees, her hands behind her back and head up but eyes looking down. John slowly moved the hair from her shoulder and lowered the cigarette. Claudia flinched as she watched him roll the glowing end across the sensitive skin where her neck met her shoulder - but Claudia showed more reaction than Max. Her only reaction was a slight stiffening of the spine. He lifted the cigarette and took a drag before lowering it towards her breast. He rolled it down her flesh, allowing it to hover just above her hardened nipple. Tears appeared in the corners of Max's eyes but she never made a sound.

'Hold it on the other nipple for a count of three,' Faith ordered.

Max's eyes widened and her teeth clenched together as she anticipated the action. Claudia had to look away but she still heard Faith say, 'One ... two ...' the pause seemed to last forever, '... three.'

Claudia looked back to see John raise the cigarette to his lips. Tears rolled down Max's cheeks and a muscle pulsed in her jaw where she was clenching her teeth so hard - but there was no other reaction.

'And now the whip,' Faith commanded.

'Which one?' John asked as he approached a chest of drawers that was similar to the one in Claudia's room. He pulled the drawer open and lifted out a long riding crop, showing it to Faith.

The mistress shook her head, 'No, the next one I think and bring those anal beads that Max loves so much.'

Nodding as he returned the first whip, John retrieved another from the drawer. This one looked like three riding crops tied together. The three lengths of braided leather were far more rigid than a usual stranded whip but were suppler than a crop. He held the whip in one hand while he slipped the top drawer open and removed a line of plastic beads. Claudia had seen anal beads before but never ones as big as these. The smallest bead at the end of the line of seven was as big as any that she had seen. The other beads along the length grew steadily in size, the largest was some two inches in diameter.

'Give her the first three,' Faith announced as John returned to the slave.

'Hands and knees,' he ordered and then knelt behind her. He spat on his fingers, rubbing the spittle around the star of her anus before spitting onto his palm and using that to lubricate the first beads on the line. He used his thumb and forefinger to part her buttocks and then inserted the first bead. Max's fingers dug into the carpet and a tiny ripple ran down her spine. The second and third beads were inserted and the only reaction from Max was a slight arching of her back. The rest of the beads were left to hang from her anus, sticking out like some strange tail.

'On your knees, hands on your head,' John commanded.

Max moved easily despite the large plastic spheres that had stretched her anus. She rested on her knees, placing her hands on top of her head with her elbows out. She arched her back, making her breasts prominent.

John raised the whip to shoulder height, took a breath and then brought the whip down. As he delivered the blow to her breasts he breathed out, increasing the strength of the blow. Max sunk under the weight and power of the blow - but she made no sound. Fresh tears sprung into her eyes and her lips were pulled tight but that was all. As he continued to deliver the terrible lashes to her breasts, her lips pulled back from her teeth and her eyes half closed - but there was no sound, no real reaction. He dispensed ten terrible blows to her breasts that rippled and swung under the punishment, quickly becoming bruised and swollen, as well as wet with the fall of tears.

'Give her the next three and then beat her arse,' Faith ordered.

Claudia made a sound that drew Faith's harsh stare and she fell silent. She had wanted to say that Faith had made her point but the mistress clearly intended John to give a full demonstration. When Claudia looked back at Max she was on her hands and knees again and John was pushing the next three beads into her arse. He had made her turn so that her buttocks were in Claudia's line of sight, allowing her to see the glistening swell of the slave's pussy beneath the remaining bead. Max's buttocks quivered as she anticipated the first cruel blow. When it fell, it landed with such strength that Max almost fell forward. Her buttocks, still red from that morning's punishment, were suddenly marked with three white lines that stood out starkly. Those lines quickly turned a pale shade of purple and lifted up from the skin. The next blow landed, crossing the first from the other direction and bringing three raised, purple crosses to her cheeks. By the time John had beaten her several more times, her buttocks were swollen and terribly bruised while the pussy beneath had opened and juice was dribbling down her thighs.

'Now fuck her - make her come.' Faith commanded as she lit herself a cigarette.

John cast the whip aside, freed himself from his trousers and sank to his knees behind the slave. He positioned his penis and slid easily into her sopping cunt, thrusting violently and almost knocking her down as he had when he had started whipping her. Max closed her eyes and gritted her teeth. Sweat rolled down her temples as she slowly moved her head from side to side.

'She's so fucking wide and wet,' John laughed, 'I can

just about feel her.'

Faith smiled, 'Don't worry, she can feel you. Give her the last bead.'

He paused in his fucking to slide the last, and thickest bead, into her stretched anus. As it slid in Max hung her head, her pussy lips spasming around his cock.

'Now, fuck her hard.'

John grabbed the slave's hips and dragged her back onto his cock, his own hips slamming against her bruised buttocks. Max's fingernails dug into the carpet, the muscles in her arms bunching and quivering. Feeling her juices building around his cock, John took hold of the ring that remained sticking out of her arse. 'She's gonna come any second,' he announced and started to pull on the beads.

'Not yet,' Faith commanded, leaning forward to watch Max. Claudia had no idea what she was looking at since Max was hardly making any reaction. John continued to drill his cock into her until Max's shoulders suddenly stiffened. 'Now.' Faith smiled.

Holding the plastic ring again, John quickly yanked the beads from her arse. Max threw her head back, her lips pulled back and her eyes screwed tightly shut. A quiver ran the length of her body as her juices splattered John's thighs.

'That will do,' Faith announced as John started to fuck the slave again.

He looked at her, his eyes heavy and aroused.

'Take her to your room and enjoy yourself,' Faith told him as she stubbed out her cigarette.

'Thank you, Mistress.' He stood quickly, fastening his trousers. Then he bent to grab the whip, the beads and finally Max.

Faith watched in silence as the door closed behind Max and John. There were several long silent seconds before

Faith slowly turned to Claudia. 'So, you see?'

Claudia nodded slowly.

'Max is my special slave. Natalie would have complimented her perfectly.'

'Why?'

'Because they are the two sides of you, my darling,' Faith replied. 'Can't you see it? Natalie is so close to succumbing - just like you. But, like Max, you never let anyone see what you are feeling. You hide your pain and your pleasure from everyone around you. Must you hide it from me too?'

Claudia stood up, 'I could never be your slave.'

'I don't want you as my slave. I just want you. That's all I ever wanted,' Faith sighed. 'As wonderful as they are, Max and Natalie are poor substitutes for you.'

'I don't believe that.'

'They are good slaves but -'

'No, I mean that I don't believe that you have been trying to find a replacement for me.'

Faith shrugged, 'When have I ever lied to you?'

'I think you're constantly lying,' Claudia announced harshly, she was sick of Faith's mind games and believed that she had started to understand the young mistress. 'I was scared of you, I admit it. But it wasn't you I was scared of - like everyone around us, I was scared of your reputation.' She took a step forward, strengthened by her own words, 'But you know what? I've not seen you lay one finger on a slave. You have your Masters to do that for you and now I understand why. You're as afraid of facing up to the truth as I am. You're not a mistress, Faith, you never were. You haven't got the strength or the power to raise a whip to a slave. It's all mind games and manipulation.'

Faith stared at her in silence but there was a dark anger glinting behind her eyes.

'I think that you're clever and you use your ability to manipulate people. Any power that you have is because of that. Strip away your reputation and there's nothing but fear.'

'Are you finished?' Faith spoke quietly and there was a terrible danger in her voice.

Claudia tried desperately to hold on to what she had said, to believe her own words. They stared at each other for endless seconds before Faith turned on her heel and left the room.

Claudia breathed heavily, adrenalin coursing through her veins. She'd done it! She'd actually done it! She had faced up to the all-powerful Faith and had actually won! She tried to calm her emotions and had managed to ease her rapidly beating heart just as the door opened and Faith entered. The breath caught in Claudia's throat when she saw the slave that Faith dragged into the room. Claudia recognised her instantly despite the fact that the slave was bent double, her hair twisted in Faith's fist. Hannah. Faith looked at Claudia as she dragged the unfortunate slave towards the bed and then, showing surprising strength, Faith threw her onto the mattress. The slave rolled onto her knees, her hands clasped behind her back and her head bowed. Tears rolled down her cheeks as she gasped, 'Mistress, what have I done?'

Faith ignored her as she turned towards the chest of drawers. She pulled the first draw open, yanking it from its housing and spilling the contents across the floor. She did the same with the second draw, spilling the assortment of whips, canes and paddles amongst the multitude of dildos, vibrators, butt plugs and other sex-toys. Faith kicked the objects into a pile and then bent to select a wide leather paddle.

'Hands and knees,' Faith ordered as she approached the bed.

Still weeping, Hannah moved into position, hanging her head between her arms.

'Put your face on the bed, lift your fucking arse!'

The slave did so. Her sobbing muffled by the mattress.

Faith lifted the paddle across her chest and then brought it slashing round to strike Hannah's buttock. The slave's knees lifted off the bed with the force of the blow and she tipped her head back to scream loudly.

'Put your fucking head … down!' Faith yelled, following the last word with another harsh smack with the paddle.

Sobbing even louder, Hannah dropped her face into the covers that were quickly become soaked with her tears.

Faith delivered ten harsh, stinging smacks with the paddle from the right side of the bed before moving to the other side and delivering another ten. The slave was racked by sobs that shook her entire body as the last echoes of the spanking died away. Faith turned from her, throwing the paddle onto the pile and then walking over to study the objects. She selected a large butt-plug and even larger vibrator that she carried back to the bed. Sparing no thought for the slave, Faith parted her glowing buttocks and drove the plug into her tight anus. Hannah screamed loudly and tried to claw her way up the bed but Faith grabbed her thighs and dragged her back, forcing the last few inches of plug into her arse. With the plug firmly inserted, Faith turned the dial of the vibrator to on and drove the trembling phallus into Hannah's cunt. The slave cried out loudly. Her cry, although from pain, was deeper than before and her gasps were for more than just discomfort.

'Kneel,' Faith ordered as she once again returned to the pile. The slave moved slowly, painfully, desperate not to lose either phallus, knowing instinctively that, that would bring about worse punishment. 'Hands on your head … chest forward.' Faith commanded as she rooted through the pile on the floor until she found a matching pair of clamps. Hannah closed her eyes as she watched the Mistress approach. 'Why are you closing your fucking eyes?' Faith demanded, harshly slapping her breast, 'Look down and see what I am doing to your titties, you fucking slut.'

Stifling a sob, Hannah looked down and was forced to watch as Faith lifted her right nipple between the two plates on the clamp and then slowly tightened the screw, squeezing the jaws together.

'Oh, God!' Hannah gasped as her nipples were crushed unbearably.

'Pathetic,' Faith hissed. 'Fucking pathetic.' She tightened the clamp with a few more turns, ignoring the slave's pitiful whimpers. She added the second clamp, tightening it as much as the first and shaking her head at the slave's hissing gasps. 'You are so fucking weak.'

She lowered her hand between the slave's legs and turned the vibrator up. When she pulled her hand free, her fingers glistened wetly. She stared at the moisture, 'Weak,' she hissed, shaking her head. She jumped off the bed and moved to retrieve a thin cane from the pile. Hannah's eyes widened as she watched Faith approach. 'What's the matter with you, slave?' Faith asked, tapping the cane against her palm.

'Please, Mistress, whatever I've done, I'm sorry.'

'And?'

'And I won't do it again … Mistress.'

Faith tipped her head slightly to the side, 'How can you not do it again when you don't even know what you've done wrong?'

Hannah swallowed, 'Mistress, if you could just tell me what I've done then … ahh!'

The cane snapped down across her breasts, half an inch above her harshly clamped nipples. 'Pardon?' Faith asked, her voice dangerously quietly.

'If … you could tell me … Mistress … what … ahh!'

Another snap as the cane found her breasts. Two white lines stretched across the pale flesh, quickly turning red. Faith returned to the pile and picked up a ball-gag. Climbing onto the bed behind Hannah, she forced the ball between her lips and then fastened the buckles tightly.

'Do you know what you are, slave?' Faith asked, leaning forward to speak directly into her ear, 'You are fucking stupid!' Faith bent her head and sank her teeth into the sensitive area at edge of Hannah's neck and shoulder. The slave struggled but Faith held her arms tightly, sucking and biting. When she lifted her head that was a livid purple bruise surrounding harsh indentations made by her teeth. Hannah sobbed against the gag, sweat rolling down her face to mix with her tears.

Faith leapt off the bed, holding the cane against her shoulder. 'Only a stupid slave would dare to tell me what to do,' she announced and delivered several lashes to her breasts. 'But on top of that …' she delivered another blow, '… only a stupid fucking slave …' swish … snap '… would assume that they had done something wrong in order to receive a punishment.' swish … snap 'This,' swish … snap 'is not a punishment for anything you have done.' swish … snap 'It is merely to remind you of your place. You are a slave,' swish … snap 'and as such you will be abused as I see fit, when I choose, regardless of what you may or may not have done wrong.' swish … snap 'I suggest that you nod to show that you understand me.'

Hannah nodded furiously, her red eyes wide and filled with pain and fear … and something else.

'Good.' Faith lashed her a few more times and then leant forward to turn the vibrator onto full power. The slave shivered uncontrollably, her thighs quivering as the phallus hummed deep in her pussy. Faith cast the cane aside and grabbed another, slimmer vibrator. Returning to the bed she turned the second phallus to full power and slid it between Hannah's thighs, searching out her clitoris. Hannah jolted as if struck by electricity and Faith knew that the phallus had found its mark. Hannah was weeping openly, groans and sobs echoing from behind the gag and making her throat pulsate and her tits shake. 'You have my permission to come,' Faith announced matter-of-factly, pressing the second phallus in harder. The scream that tore at Hannah's throat was stifled by the gag but was no less piercing. Her whole body quivered violently and then went suddenly rigid. The slave fell backward and Faith let her go, riding the movement to keep the phallus pushed against her clitoris. Hannah gave one final, stifled cry and fell completely limp.

It was several moments before Claudia found the strength to take a deep breath. She had stumbled back against the wall at some point and now she could feel herself sliding down that wall to the floor, tears rolling down her cheeks. Her hands were shaking and her breathing was harsh and ragged. She hardly noticed when the door opened and an unknown man entered to remove the slave.

Faith and Claudia locked stares for several, silent minutes.

It was Faith who spoke first, 'Never underestimate me again.'

'Is that all that fucking was?' Claudia cried, her anger giving her the strength to get to her feet. 'You did all those things to that girl just to prove a point to me?

Faith stared at her in silence. Eventually she replied, 'You challenged me. I would recommend that you don't ever do that again.'

'Is that a threat?'

'It's a statement of fact.'

Claudia threw her arms in the air, 'What gives you the right to behave like this?'

'I told you, this is my world.' Faith slowly walked over to Claudia. 'And you can act as upset as you like but I know the truth.'

'And what is that?'

'You're more upset that you were not that slave. You'd love me to abuse you like that.'

Claudia shook her head, 'No.'

'Yes,' Faith moved fast, grabbing Claudia's arms and pushing her back against the wall. She held her firmly with her own body, forcing her thigh between Claudia's legs. 'You're wet right now,' Faith whispered into Claudia's hair. 'You're wet and you're aroused. You'd love me to whip you almost as much as you're desperate for me to fuck you.'

Claudia gave a small, angry cry and grabbed Faith's arms, pushing her away. But then she looked into those deep brown eyes and she was suddenly drowning in them. She fell into those eyes, her mouth finding Faith's and feeding hungrily on her lust and power. She tasted Faith's arousal and her head swam as her body screamed for release.

Faith tore at her clothes with a hunger that matched her own. She didn't even try to unfasten the buttons of her blouse, she just tore the material open and forced her hands up between them, kneading Claudia's breasts. Claudia pushed herself against those rough hands. Faith's fingers pushed under the bra and clasped the naked flesh beneath, making Claudia hiss as she rolled her nipples

93

between thumb and forefinger. Faith responded to Claudia's hiss of pain by sucking on her tongue, her teeth nibbling at the organ. Claudia felt her knees weaken and she tried to hold on to Faith. Noticing the other woman's reaction, Faith stumbled backwards, taking Claudia with her. They reached the bed and fell, Faith managing to turn Claudia so that she landed on top of her. She broke from the kiss and grabbed Claudia's wrists in one hand, forcing her arms above her head as she tore the bra down her breasts. She growled as she bent her mouth to the smooth mounds, sucking and nibbling at the flesh. She rose up again, grabbing one of Claudia's breasts with her free hand and digging her nails into the sensitive flesh. Claudia gasped and arched her back, shaking her head. 'Please, Faith, I don't want that.'

'Yes, you do,' Faith whispered, gripping the breast harder and making Claudia cry out.

'No,' Claudia half cried but any protest was cut off by Faith who smothered her mouth with her own and drove her thigh up between Claudia's legs. Claudia arched her back and cried out against Faith's mouth, but this time it was with sheer hunger. She ground her soaking pussy onto Faith's leg, feeling the material of her panties and trousers forming a barrier between her need and her release. Faith sensed her desire and reached back to pull at the fastening of Claudia's trousers. When she found that she couldn't do it with one hand, she jumped off the bed and moved to the pile of sex-toys. Claudia groaned with desire, closing her eyes and running her hands through her hair. Suddenly her hands were grabbed again and she felt cold metal encircle her wrists. Her eyes snapped open and she stared fearfully at Faith as the handcuffs closed around her wrists, locking them together. Her arms were dragged upwards and another pair of handcuffs fixed her wrists to a metal ring secured to the headboard of the bed.

'Faith,' Claudia whispered, hearing fear and lust fill her voice in equal measure.

The young Mistress stared at her, her eyes shining with lust and desire. She smiled, a soft, gentle smile that would have been alien on the Mistress' face had Claudia not seen it before. For a brief moment it was like looking at the Faith that she had loved. But then those hard, experienced hands tore at her clothes in a way that was alien and all Claudia could do was trust that Faith still felt enough for her not to hurt her. The idea that she was at Faith's mercy, and the fear that it brought, was intoxicating and fuelled her desire. Faith tore the material of Claudia's trousers, dragging them from her legs with harsh pulls. Her blouse, bra and panties went the same way. And then she was naked beneath Faith's all-powerful stare. Faith's gaze was like a flame that warmed her entire body, awakening her nerve endings and making her head swim.

'Oh God …' Claudia whispered, '… fuck me.'

Faith's lip curled in a smile, 'How, my darling?'

'I don't care … just make me come!'

Faith's nails found Claudia's breasts again and this time, as Claudia arched her back, she cried out in pleasure and pain. Her nipples were harshly pinched and Claudia had a sudden flash of the clamps that had cruelly squashed Hannah's hard nipples. The vision made her pussy spasm and she thought that she would climax right there and then but Faith's nails dug into her inner thighs, making her scream. Those nails scratched their way up her inner thigh until they pressed at her vagina lips, pinching the swollen labia and brushing her aching clitoris. She felt her juices soaking Faith's hand and she bucked her hips up, desperate to feel her fingers searching inside her. She cried out in disappointment when that hand was gone from her pussy and she raised her head to search for the young Mistress.

Faith stood just off to the side, watching Claudia as she slowly undressed. She shed her clothes like a skin, letting the material pool around her feet. When she was naked she let Claudia drink in the sight of her tanned, lithe body. If anything she was more beautiful than Claudia remembered. Faith walked slowly to the bed and climbed on beside Claudia, swinging her leg over Claudia's chest and crawling up the bed until her pussy hovered over Claudia's face. Claudia inhaled her musky scent and her mind swam with the sheer familiarity of it. Suddenly she gasped as Faith grabbed a handful of her hair and pulled her head up. Faith twisted her fingers in the raven hair, causing pain to lance across Claudia's scalp as the soaking, plump pussy lips smothered her mouth. She tensed and Faith eased her hold a little, gasping loudly as Claudia took her first taste of that beautiful cunt. She licked her way between the labia lips, pushing at the clitoris with her teeth and then dragging her teeth down again to force her tongue into the wide hole beneath. Faith ground her cunt onto Claudia's probing tongue, gasping as her aroused pussy responded to the touch. It was but a few moments before the mistress climaxed with a small cry, her fingers twisting Claudia's hair painfully as her juice gushed into her mouth.

Breathing heavily, Faith slowly slipped off Claudia and moved to the pile of toys. Claudia watched her as she bent and retrieved something. Keeping her back to Claudia, Faith slipped a belt around her waist and fastened it. When she turned Claudia's eyes widened at the sight of the thick, black dildo that protruded from Faith's groin. She felt her breath freeze in her throat as Faith bent again and retrieved a string of anal beads - smaller but not dissimilar to the ones that John had used on Max. Again, a vision swam through her mind that made her pussy spasm. Faith licked along the length of the anal beads as she slowly approached the bed. She climbed on the end and leant forward to grip Claudia's hips.

'Roll over,' Faith said, her voice strong and authoritative.

Claudia wanted to refuse but not as much as she wanted to feel those anal beads sliding home. She rolled over, moving her arms so that the handcuffs attached to the headboard twisted. Faith helped her to get to her knees and Claudia rested her head against the mattress. She felt the mistress' fingers parting her buttocks and the first smooth bead pressed against the star of her anus. She gasped as the pressure opened her hole and the bead slipped in, her anus closing behind it. The next, larger bead, was slid home and then the next. Claudia found herself counting each of the beads as it entered her with that delicious feeling of invasion. Nine beads in all were slid into her rectum and Claudia circled her hips, sighing at the wonderful feeling of her arse being filled. She heard herself cry out as the tip of the thick dildo found her pussy. Claudia held her breath as slowly, inch by inch, the dildo slid into her welcoming cunt. Her pussy swallowed it easily, grasping at the rubber and sucking it deep. Faith held her buttocks, pushing against them as she pulled free. The tip of the dildo slid from her cunt, leaving her feeling empty. But the feeling didn't last and soon the dildo was sliding back in. This time, when Faith withdrew, she dug her nails into Claudia's buttocks as she slowly pulled back.

'Oh God, please just fuck me,' Claudia nearly screamed. The slow moving dildo was making her head swim and her abdomen cramped with unspent lust.

Faith slowly slid the dildo back in, her hand resting

on Claudia's buttock. When the dildo was buried deep inside her, Faith delivered a stinging slap to Claudia's buttock, making the flesh shiver. Claudia cried out, thrusting her hips back against Faith. Another slap and Claudia screamed, another and another. The stinging blows drove Claudia wild and soon she was begging Faith to fuck her, tears rolling from her eyes as she pleaded for release. Faith gripped her hips, digging her nails into the flesh as she pulled Claudia back onto the thrusting dildo. The cuffs jangled as her bound wrists were tugged against the restraints. Faith fucked her furiously, drilling her as deep and as hard as she could. Sweat dripped between her breasts, running down her stomach and mingling with Claudia's juices.

'Oh fuck!' Claudia screamed, throwing her head back and pushing herself back against Faith. Her orgasm struck with a sudden, unrelenting wave of pleasure that nearly knocked Claudia senseless. She cried out, over and over as her orgasm reached its peak and then, as her pleasure crested, Faith yanked the beads from her arse. Claudia cried out as if in agony but it was the complete opposite. Quivering violently, Claudia fell forward onto the bed, weeping softly as her pussy dribbled the last drips of her spent lust.

*

Claudia sat up, the smooth sheet falling around her thighs. She found a packet of cigarettes in the bedside table and lit one with shaking hands before dropping the packet in her lap. A few moments later she felt the bed move and she watched as Faith's fingers searched out the cigarettes and the lighter. The smell of a second cigarette filled the room and Claudia tensed as she felt the smoke rolling over the scars on her back. She didn't need to look over her shoulder to know that Faith was studying the thin lines. She tensed again as she felt Faith's finger trace along the lines of the scars, the heat from the cigarette was close but didn't hurt. Warm smoke curled around her shoulder blades.

'Have you forgiven me yet?' Faith asked softly.

Claudia glanced over her shoulder, staring at the young mistress as the fog of time cleared from her mind, like the fading smoke from the cigarette. Suddenly she remembered it all as if it had only just happened …

… 'Guess who I just bumped into,' the words dripped with fury as Faith stood, staring coldly at Claudia. Claudia swallowed, suddenly more afraid of Faith than she had ever been of Michael.

'Faith -' Claudia began but the younger woman held her hand up, cutting her off.

'Don't,' she snarled, 'just don't.' Faith let her glare stay on Claudia for a few seconds before she turned and headed into the bedroom.

Claudia took several deep breaths before she followed. She entered the bedroom, determined to explain everything but she was suddenly grabbed and propelled towards the bed. Frozen with fear and the memory of what had happened, Claudia couldn't fight back as a gag was tied around her mouth. She was thrown face down onto the bed and her hands were hauled above her head. Her legs were spread, ankles tied separately to the legs of the bed. Claudia managed to turn her head and felt something close to relief when she realised that the only other occupant of the room was Faith. But that relief was short-lived, her terror quickly returning as Faith began to strip her. She tore at Claudia's clothes, ripping the material and yanking it away, not caring that her nails scratched Claudia's skin.

When she was naked, Faith slowly ran her hand down the smooth skin of Claudia's back. 'All healed now,' Faith whispered. 'All healed like it never happened. They never marked you ... but they marked me. He marked me.'

Claudia knew that Faith was referring to Michael and she managed to lift her head to look at the young woman. There were tears in Faith's eyes and Claudia felt a glimmer of hope. Maybe she could still stop this madness.

'You've hurt me so much,' Faith whispered painfully, 'I swore that no one would ever hurt me again.'

Claudia mumbled into the gag, desperate to make Faith understand that whatever she thought had happened - it hadn't. But Faith paid no heed and suddenly, angrily, wiped the tears from her eyes with the back of her hand. She turned and walked slowly to the wardrobe that they shared. She retrieved a small case from the bottom and, for the briefest of seconds, Claudia was suddenly terrified that Faith was about to pack her things and leave. Even tied, naked and helpless, the thought of losing Faith was more than she could bear.

Faith laid the suitcase on the floor and opened the lid. From inside she retrieved a thin, braided whip. It was the length of a riding crop but thinner and suppler. Claudia closed her eyes, she couldn't look at Faith as she approached the bed. She screwed up her eyes, gritting her teeth as she awaited the inevitable. She heard the swish of the whip and her eyes opened wide. The whip landed with a snap, flattening her buttocks in a line across the centre. It didn't hurt. Claudia could feel where the whip had landed, like a thousand needles digging into her skin - but it didn't hurt. And then the multitude of needles suddenly grew warmer as a strange cold crept up her back from the base of her spine. The heat didn't stop growing and Claudia felt herself gasping over and over as the heat became a searing line of fire that seemed to engulf her entire buttocks. The second blow fell with devastating accuracy, an inch below the first. The third blow landed an inch above the first. Claudia screamed into the gag that muffled her cries as she tossed her head and struggled against the bonds. The blows spread out parallel to that first strike, moving down the back of her thighs and up her buttocks until she was lined from knee to waist.

Faith paused then, staring at the red and white flesh that glistened with beads of sweat. 'How could you do it to me?' Faith asked, her voice desperately sad. 'How could you do it to me? … You fucking bitch!' her sadness turned to anger with startling speed and she launched a frenzied attack. Gone were the precision blows - her attack was pure fury.

Claudia's screams were horrendous, even with the gag, as the whip fell across her lower back again and again, drawing blood to the surface and eventually splitting the skin. Claudia swooned under the torrent, her head falling onto the pillow that was soaked with her tears. She could feel something warm sliding down her sides but she had no idea what is was.

Claudia was brought back to full-consciousness as she was rolled over. Her scream tore uselessly at the gag as the mattress sank beneath her. Her ankles, which had been untied while she had drifted in darkness, were tied together now and pushed up so that they rested near her buttocks. Faith pushed her legs open, exposing her pussy and sensitive inner thighs. Claudia stared up at Faith through tear-filled eyes as her lover climbed onto the bed and raised the whip. The torrent of blows fell first on her breasts and once they were red and speckled with blood, the whip fell upon her inner thighs. Weakened by the terrible abuse that she had already suffered, Claudia didn't have the strength to close her legs and could only suffer under the torrent of blows. The whip found her pussy last and Claudia swooned again as her entire body was engulfed in flame.

Claudia stirred as she felt the mattress sink under another's weight. She felt something nudge her bruised pussy and then she screamed uselessly as a thick dildo was driven into her. With her legs opened as they were, Claudia was speared deeply and she sobbed against the gag as Faith's weight fell upon her. Faith lay on her for several seconds before she suddenly reared up and began to fuck Claudia harshly. Her bruised pussy burned terribly, the welts on her back burning anew as her body was pushed back and forth. Above her, Faith grunted as if she could feel something herself. The sound of Faith's pleasure made Claudia gasp and suddenly her pussy spasmed with lust, contracting around the spearing phallus. She threw her head back, screaming as loudly behind the gag as when the whip had found her pussy lips. Suddenly she bucked her hips involuntarily, nearly throwing Faith off. But the younger woman forced her back down with a grinding, piercing thrust that sent shudders through them both. And then Claudia was lost to the tide of unbelievable pleasure that was almost as painful in its intensity. Faith rode the waves of Claudia's climax, drilling as deeply into her as she could and forcing every last ounce of pleasure from her. It was then that Claudia succumbed completely and let the darkness take her.

When she awoke, free of her bonds and covered by the sheets, Faith was gone ...

Claudia jumped as she felt Faith's hand touching her own. She looked down and realised that the young mistress was taking the burnt out cigarette from her fingers. Claudia climbed from the bed and approached the window. She was stunned to realise that it was dark

102

outside.

'Can't you answer my question?' Faith asked from the bed.

Claudia stared at the mistress' reflection in the window. Slowly she shook her head. 'No,' she whispered, 'I can't answer you.'

'Can't or won't?'

'Can't,' Claudia replied flatly.

'Why not?'

She turned slowly, 'Because you're not the person who gave me these scars. You're not the woman I loved.'

Faith stared at her, 'You loved the woman who hurt you?'

Claudia was annoyed by Faith's attempt to twist things. To avoid answering she asked, 'Why did you leave?'

'After what happened I decided that, that would be what you wanted,' Faith replied. 'And I was right, wasn't I?'

'You didn't give me a chance. You never gave me a chance.'

'To do what? To spin some lies about your precious Michael and what he was doing at the flat?'

'No. You should have given me the chance to explore what you wanted to show me.'

Faith looked genuinely confused but eventually she said, 'You weren't ready to join me.'

'Maybe you should have given me more time.'

'You're not even ready now, are you?'

'I'll never be ready to join you in this world,' Claudia sighed.

'I don't believe that.'

'You have to. If this is your world then there is no room in it for me.'

'I'll always leave a space for you,' Faith announced, she sounded almost desperate.

103

'It will remain empty,' Claudia whispered.

'Damn you,' Faith snarled. 'The only person you're kidding is yourself.'

'I'll live with that if it means that I'm the only person that I'm hurting.'

Faith looked as if she wanted to say something but stopped herself, 'I'll get us some food.'

After they had eaten, Faith moved the tray to the floor and slowly ran her hand up Claudia's thigh. Claudia wanted to push her hand away but she couldn't and Faith fell onto her, smothering Claudia's mouth with her own.

CHAPTER 1.5:

Claudia awoke with a start, dark dreams clinging to the beads of sweat running down her spine as she sat up. She took a deep breath and tried to steady her rapidly beating heart. Someone stirred beside her and she looked over her shoulder. She saw Faith and the sleep-induced clouds fell from her mind as she realised that the dark dreams, from which she had awoken, had followed her. She shifted, gasping as her bruised buttocks pressed into the mattress. Faith and Claudia had made love several times during the night and each time Faith's playful spankings grew steadily stronger. At the time the warmth that had smothered her buttocks had been a pleasurable addition to the lust - but now, in the cold light of morning …

Angry with herself and not really sure why, Claudia swung her legs out of the bed and stood up. She lit herself a cigarette and paced the room, inhaling smoke deep into her lungs and exhaling as a sigh. She finished the cigarette and lit another before continuing with her pacing. She stopped when she felt someone watching her and turned slowly towards the bed. Even when she had just woken Faith still had that deep intensity in her eyes. Claudia remembered waking up to that stare and recalled how it had always warmed her deep to her core. It was as if Faith could stare into her and see all the deepest secrets, even the ones that she hid from herself. A long time ago it had been almost exciting for Faith to have that power, but now Faith was using that power against her and Claudia didn't like it. She didn't like this new, powerful Faith and was afraid of her. But even so, despite her anger and fear, she couldn't hide from the fact that, in some respects, Faith hadn't changed at all. She still had the ability to make Claudia feel so alive.

The previous night had only served to show her how much she had missed the young woman, how much she had longed to feel alive again even though she had never realised how empty and dead she had really been feeling. It was a terrible mixture and conflict of emotions that Claudia just wasn't ready to deal with. Perhaps sensing this, Faith slowly sat up.

'I think we should have some breakfast.'

Claudia's stomach rumbled at the mention of food and she nodded with the barest of smiles. 'I'll just get showered and dressed.'

'You look fine to me.'

Claudia gave a tiny smile in response before turning for the door. She didn't feel like collecting her clothes that had been torn and scattered around the floor. Instead she prayed that she didn't meet anyone in the hallway and pulled the door open. She showered and dressed in time for Faith to appear and they went downstairs together.

They ate a huge breakfast in comfortable silence. Afterwards Faith stood and led Claudia out onto the veranda where, just twenty-four hours earlier, Max had been beaten. She put the memories of the previous morning to the back of her mind as she followed Faith down the stone steps and onto the smooth, landscaped lawn.

It was a beautiful sunny morning and Claudia revelled in the feel of the sun on her face. Everything was so peaceful and quiet. She remembered simpler times indeed - but would she have exchanged them for her life now? She doubted it.

They walked in silence for several minutes before Faith asked softly, 'If I give you time, will you come back to me?'

Claudia paused, considering the question that a part

of her had been expecting. 'I won't be your slave,' she replied eventually.

'I told you - I don't want you as my slave,' Faith replied as she turned to face Claudia, that intensity in her eyes was as brilliant as ever, 'But you still need to be someone's slave - you can't hide from that forever. You played the Mistress for Strick but we both know that's not you. When will you admit it? You can't hide forever.'

Claudia couldn't deny Faith's words, instead she said, 'I can try.'

'No one can hide from what they are and what they feel. Not you, not Max, not Natalie. Max accepts what she is, I almost had Natalie do the same. Must you make me turn my attentions on you?'

Claudia stared at her in silence, anger and fear coursing through her veins.

'You can't hide forever.'

'But that's the point, Faith, that isn't your choice to make.'

'It's always about choice with you,' Faith responded. 'That's the difference between you and me. Your life has always been about choice and you can't bear the thought of losing that.'

'And what?' Claudia challenged. 'Your life has been about not having choices? You seemed to make plenty of choices when you were with me.'

Anger flowed in Faith's eyes, 'Don't tell me what I've had in my life - you know nothing.' The anger faded quickly, 'Let's just enjoy the moment then.'

Claudia nodded slowly as they started walking again. Up ahead Claudia could see a beautiful, white summerhouse. She was about to comment on it when she realised that they were heading in that direction.

The summerhouse was even more beautiful close up. Made entirely of white marble, it looked both warm and cold at the same time. It was almost a living thing. Six columns, standing on carved plinths atop a smooth circular base supported the ceiling and domed roof. Within those columns were three curved benches that ran around the edge of the base. A space of perhaps nine feet in diameter was held within and held between the front two columns was Max. Her wrists were tied with leather cord, stretched high above her head, the cord of leather disappeared to fix to the column somewhere out of sight. Her ankles were tied similarly with her legs stretched apart, the tendons along her inner thighs straining like steel cables. The tanned skin of her naked, stretched form should have been a sharp contrast against the white marble - but it wasn't. Her body, toned and brown, looked perfect between the columns as if she were an integral part of the summerhouse itself. The summerhouse, warm and alive, seemed to wear Max. It was a strikingly erotic view that Claudia would have been drawn to even if Faith hadn't taken her hand and led her towards the scene. Any words of anger that had passed between Claudia and Faith were forgotten. The sight before her set something burning deep in Claudia's gut and she was intoxicated by both the sight of the tied slave and the feel of Faith beside her.

Max watched them approach through heavily lidded eyes and as they drew nearer Claudia noticed the rapid rise and fall of the slave's chest. The slave's inner thighs glistened and Claudia realised that the slave was severely aroused. She couldn't help but wonder how long the slave had been tied here, every passing moment increasing her slavish passions. As her eyes drank in the scene, she noticed the black dial almost hidden in the folds of Max's pussy and the cause of Max's barely contained lust was made apparent. Keeping hold of Claudia's hand, Faith walked past Max and stood in the centre of the summerhouse. Turning slowly, Claudia managed to stifle a gasp as she stared at the slave. A vibrator, as thick as anything Claudia had seen, was barely showing from between her buttocks. Now that she was closer, Claudia could hear the gentle hum as the two phalluses worked inside her. But what was incredible was that there was no apparent means of keeping those vibrators inside the slave's body. Faith perhaps sensed Claudia's amazement because she gave a small laugh and said, 'She's holding them all by herself - isn't she magnificent?'

Claudia nodded dumbly - what could she say that wouldn't betray the tremors she was feeling.

'Do you know that she can make a man come just by using her pelvic muscles?' Faith smiled, 'I know quite a few men who pay well for that.'

Claudia stared at the young mistress, her lust draining away when she heard Faith speaking of prostituting the slave.

'Oh, don't look so shocked. Did you think that this summerhouse was from MFI?'

'How can you do it?' Claudia whispered. 'How can you treat people like this?'

Faith sighed, suddenly tired and angry, 'Because it makes me wet.'

Claudia was stunned by the response and she stared at Faith, her mouth hanging open, as the young mistress stepped into her. She didn't pull away as Faith moved her face to Claudia's neck, her breath was hot and danced along her skin as she spoke, 'And it makes you wet too.'

Claudia swallowed.

'What would you give to have me take that whore down and string you up instead?' Faith whispered, 'I won't hurt you, but I will fuck you while you are so beautifully restrained. I'll lick and finger you until you scream for me to make you come … and then I'll stop and let you cool a little before I start again. I'll keep you going all day and then, as the sun sets, I'll make you come so hard that you'll want to scream and never stop.'

Claudia dropped to her knees, Faith following her down. Her breath was harsh in her throat, her chest heaving with lust. Faith unfastened the button of her jeans and pulled the material down her legs, taking her soaking panties with them. She slipped her socks and shoes off too and let her naked buttocks lie against the cold marble. It was an amazing feeling and Claudia gasped as the cold seemed to seize her entire body but it was a strange cold and Claudia wanted to remove every last bit of clothing so that she could feel it all over her. Faith helped her, carefully removing her blouse. She wore no bra beneath and she gave a small cry as she lay back on the marble floor and let that strange coldness envelop her. Faith gently parted her legs, tracing a line down the inside of her thighs with her fingernails. Her fingers stroked at the plump, moist pussy lips and Claudia closed her eyes, biting her bottom lip. 'John,' Faith said, startling Claudia.

'Mistress?' he asked as he stepped from behind a pillar.

Claudia stared at him as he looked down at her and she knew that she was looking at him through the same, heavy-lidded eyes, with which Max had looked at her.

'I want you to beat the slave,' Faith announced, her fingers working expertly at Claudia's pussy, keeping her passions mounting. It was a cruel trick because Faith knew how to ensure that Claudia's lust prevented her from saying anything that might stop the pleasant stroking. 'But first, I want you to turn those vibrators up to full. If the whore wants to come, then she may come.' Faith spoke loud enough for Max to hear her, 'If she can hold onto those false dicks inside her while you beat her buttocks and breasts, then I'm sure she will have a quite delightful climax. If she loses them, well ...' the mistress sighed sadly, '... then she will just have to wait until I am ready to finish her off myself.'

John nodded and slipped the ever-present crop from his belt. He approached Max with a smile creasing his lips. He turned the dials on the vibrators and the humming grew louder and more insistent. Claudia noticed the tension that suddenly shot along the slave's stretched arms and legs - but the slave herself made no sound. He began by beating her buttocks with stinging blows - one across and then the second on the back swing. Tremors ran up her back and seemed to encompass her whole body. Claudia lay with her head turned towards the slave, watching those tremors as Faith's hand worked at her pussy lips. She wanted to tell John to stop, wanted to beg him to leave the slave alone - but if she did then she knew that Faith would stop that pleasant teasing and, god help her, she couldn't let her. A small tear collected in the corner of Claudia's eye and then, as John moved round to start beating Max's breasts, that tear rolled down the side of her face to become lost in her hair. Faith's finger pressed against her clitoris and Claudia cried out, arching her back. 'Oh God!' she almost screamed.

Faith leant into her, 'What do you want my darling?'

Claudia was almost crying, 'I want you to fuck me ... I need you to fuck me.'

There was a clatter from beside them and Claudia turned to see the two vibrators rolling across the marble floor. She looked up and saw Max's head hanging down, tiny quivers running back and forth across her buttocks and shoulder blades. A line of white juice was sliding down Max's inner thigh.

'Oh, fuck me now!' this time Claudia did scream and Faith laughed as she lifted her up and threw her over one of the marble benches. Claudia let her breasts be squashed painfully against the cold marble and then she

111

threw her head back and screamed as Faith's mouth found her cunt. The mistress' tongue slid along the groove of her sex, up and then down to press against the hard nub of her clitoris. Claudia screamed again and then her head fell forward as Faith slid her tongue between the swollen lips. Her delicious, moist tongue slid into her soaking vagina and she gasped as her muscles clenched. Faith's hands stroked her buttocks, her nails pressing at the small bruises from the previous night and Claudia yelped with delight. Something touched her face and she looked up, her eyes widening as she stared up at John who was naked and hard before her. He smiled, pushing his thick prick towards her lips. Claudia reared back, shaking her head. His lips curled in a snarl of anger and for a moment Claudia feared that he would force her to take him in her mouth. His eyes flashed with fury and he took a sharp step back. Claudia lost him from view and she glanced over her shoulder to see him approach Max. The slave raised her head as she felt his cock nudging between her buttocks and then he slammed into her with all that fury that had shone in his eyes. Claudia felt a wave of guilt wash over her but it was chased away by Faith's lips and tongue as she continued to work at her cunt. Claudia gasped and hung her head again, trying to shut out the sound of John's violent fucking. Faith suddenly pulled back and the emptiness that she left was quickly filled by her fingers that searched deep inside Claudia, seeking out her lust and playing it like a string desperate to snap. Claudia started to cry out, tiny cries that grew louder and louder as Faith drove her to near climax and held her hanging there for an eternity before she let that wave of pleasure break over her. The power of her climax shook Claudia and brought tears to her eyes as she shuddered and slid from the marble seat. She lay, huddled and quivering, stunned by the power of her orgasm. Faith stroked her tenderly and for a few seconds there was no one but them. But then she heard John grunt and Claudia was dragged, unwillingly, back to Faith's world as she watched the slave suffering as John drove his cock into her anus and scored her flesh with his nails.

'Here.' Faith said softly, a smile creasing her full lips.

Claudia held her hand out before she realised what Faith was handing her. Only when the vibrator rested heavy against her palm did Claudia realise what it was.

'Fuck me while I watch the slave suffer,' Faith whispered as she lay back and spread her thighs.

Claudia swallowed, desperate to refuse but equally desperate to watch Faith climax beneath her hands. Slowly she turned the vibrator on to its lowest setting and dipped the phallus to Faith's pussy. The mistress jolted as it found her clitoris and a tiny gasp escaped her lips as she stared up at Max.

The slave jerked in her bonds as John climaxed inside her, her head slumping forwards as she must have felt him spurt his thick come into her, but then her head jerked back upright as John dragged himself out of her with brutal suddenness. Then he stepped back and took up the crop once more. As the thin, braided shaft sliced across the already terribly bruised and welted buttocks, incredibly Max just jerked in response. Not a sound escaped her.

'That's it, my pretty slave, suffer for me,'

*

Morning sunlight, although filtered by thick curtains, was still enough to wake Claudia. She rolled onto her back, groaning as her body protested. As she rolled Claudia realised that the bed felt strange and empty. Opening her eyes she looked at the empty half of the bed and tried to suppress a part of her that was

113

disappointed that Faith was not there. She listened to see if she could hear anything from the en-suite bathroom but the room was quiet. Claudia half sat up and it was then that she noticed the sheet of paper on Faith's dented pillow. She unfolded it, recognising Faith's curled handwriting immediately.

You looked too peaceful to wake, my darling.

I have some business to attend to in the city and I have

arranged for John to drive you wherever you wish.

I'll be at the club later tonight, meet me there and we will

discuss Natalie.

It has been an unforgettable weekend.

F x

Claudia read the note again and sighed angrily. As far as she was concerned there was nothing to discuss. She had spent the weekend with Faith, which had been her part of the deal.

The rest of the Sunday had been spent between arguing about their views on the world and pleasuring each other. Eventually Faith had ended it by saying, 'It seems that we are destined to fuck each other ... one way or another.'

That comment had hurt Claudia and it must have shown in her eyes because Faith had seemed a little sorry, even if she didn't say so. They had made love again, Faith had pinched and bitten Claudia's breasts until she had screamed in climax before falling, weeping, onto the bed. She had awoken during the night from dark dreams and had found the young mistress sleeping beside her. The closeness of another human being had been comforting, even if it had been Faith that had made her scream within her dreams. It had been Faith who had stroked her skin with the impossible long whip, Faith who had fucked her until she felt she was being turned inside out - and

114

maybe in her dream she was. She had wanted to hold Faith, to feel that closeness properly but the visions from the dream wouldn't leave her and so she had settled with her back to Faith, taking some comfort from the mistress' soft breathing. And as she had slowly drifted off to sleep again, she heard words in her head, spoken by a voice that was her own, 'This paradox can not go on.' She fell asleep before she could answer and when she awoke, Faith was not there to help her solve the problem and for that, she was grateful because she now realised that if Faith had been there, any reasoning would have been clouded by her feelings for the young mistress and everything that she was capable of doing.

Claudia sighed angrily again. Damn it, she had to get out of this house.

She washed and dressed quickly before heading downstairs. She declined breakfast and sought out John who nodded at her request to drive her back to London. While he went to get the car, Claudia managed to find a telephone and called her flat. Thankfully Mel answered.

'It's Claudia.' she announced in reply to Mel's greeting.

'Thank God. Are you okay?'

Mel sounded relieved which made Claudia smile, 'I'm fine. I'm on my way home.'

'And everything else is … sorted out?'

'Yes,' Claudia responded with conviction even though she would confirm everything with Faith that night. She glanced towards the door where John was standing, impatiently shifting from one foot to the other.

'I have to go.' she announced, 'I'll see you later.'

'Take care.'

'You too.' She put the phone down and then followed John to the car.

She sat in the back as a way of avoiding conversation and allowed her mind to replay the events of the weekend. She was so lost in thought that she was startled when the door beside her suddenly opened. 'Are we here?' she asked as she climbed out of the car with a frown.

'No.' John replied, 'We've got a flat, I'll have to change it.' He gestured towards the front tyre. Her frown deepening, Claudia approached the fully inflated tyre. She was about to ask him which wheel was flat when her vision was suddenly filled by a sharp, blinding light and then darkness.

Interlude:

A Slave meets a Mistress

The door closed at her back, closing on the world behind her and, taking a deep breath, she stepped into heavy atmosphere of the club beyond. The smell of sex and desire was tangible, the sounds all too audible as gasps, groans and stifled screams echoed from the shadows. Those sounds struck a chord deep inside her, like an alcoholic smelling a drink and feeling his dangerous appetites reawaken. Mel tried to shut out the sounds and she didn't let her eyes stray, but she couldn't rid her mouth of that familiar taste of excitement and fear. She licked her lips, part of her hungry to feast but she shook her head and followed the man.

She was led to a table in the corner of the club and the sounds of lust and pain faded to a distant echo as she stared at the woman who was sitting there. So, this was Faith. The young mistress looked up at Mel, a strange look of half recognition flashing across her eyes.

'I have to talk to you,' Mel announced, forcing strength into her voice.

'Is that right?' Faith asked, a smile playing at her lips as she saw straight through Mel's facade. 'And who might you be, my pretty slave?'

Mel swallowed, 'A friend of Claudia's.'

'And?'

'And she hasn't returned home.'

No emotion showed in Faith's eyes, her face could have been carved from marble. Silent seconds ticked by before Faith said, 'You're Mel, aren't you?'

'I came here to talk about Claudia,' Mel insisted, sitting down.

'This is my club and we shall talk about what I choose.'

Mel stared at her, trying to force strength into her voice as she replied, 'I don't have time to shoot the breeze. Are you going to help me or not?'

Faith's face turned from marble to steel in an instant. 'Who the hell do you think you're talking to?'

Mel jumped as if she had been slapped and quickly hung her head. For a moment it seemed as if Mel was going to fall to her knees at Faith's feet but she abruptly recovered and stared back at her. There was fury in her eyes but Faith knew that Mel's fury was not directed at her. Her reaction to Faith gave Mel the first inkling of just how powerful Faith was. Unlike Claudia, Mel had a deeper understanding of Faith's natural power. All of the other Mistresses and Masters that Mel had ever suffered under, had been different. They had developed and honed their skills and, for many, money had bought them the power and the chance to explore it. Faith was so different. Her power ran so much deeper. As she stared at Faith, she saw a familiarity in her stare. For Faith, the boundaries between right and wrong, between choice and force, were blurred and she stood right in the middle of that grey area. And there was the familiarity, Faith stood in that same no-man's land where she and Natalie had lived for so long.

'You can no more hide from who you truly are than I can,' Faith suddenly announced, as if reading Mel's thoughts - and perhaps she had, perhaps she had seen it all in Mel's eyes. 'I'm as much a slave to my passions as you are to yours.'

Mel's anger surfaced again, 'Except that no one forced you to become a Mistress, did they?'

A strange look passed across Faith's face as she said, 'You learnt to take pleasure in your submission in order to survive. Don't think that it doesn't work the other way. We all do what we have to do survive.' The look passed as quickly as it had come and Faith smiled, the look of a Mistress firmly in place once more.

The silence stretched on intolerably.

'Will you help me?' Mel asked quietly.

Faith raised her eyebrows, 'In what way, exactly?'

'To help me find Claudia?'

'I believe you have more immediate problems than that.'

Mel frowned.

'I can smell you,' Faith announced, 'How long has it been since you last had any release?'

Mel stared back, she wanted to be annoyed but Faith's voice had lowered and her eyes were cold and harsh - the eyes of a Mistress. She swallowed, 'Natalie pleasures me just fine, I -'

'I'm not talking about pleasure - I'm talking about release,' Faith responded. 'When was the last time you had a good thrashing?'

Mel felt her pussy contract and she shifted in her seat.

'I can see how we can help each other out.'

Mel moved to stand but her legs refused to cooperate, it was as if her feet were bolted to the floor.

'Do you want me to fuck you?' Faith asked.

'No,' Mel whispered.

Faith smiled knowingly, 'Of course not. Allowing me to fuck you would mean betraying Natalie.' The Mistress stood and stared down at Mel, 'Well, how about I force you?'

'Don't you care about Claudia?' Mel asked, trying to keep her voice from shaking.

Again that looked passed across Faith's face but was gone just as quickly. 'Now, what would the people here think if they saw me let a slave like you get away without fucking you? I do have a reputation to protect.'

Mel swallowed, she was fully aware of Faith's

reputation. 'Please … don't.'

'Stand up.' Faith ordered.

'I just want to find Claudia and know that she's alright,' Mel half cried, her voice trembling now.

'And I just want to shove my fingers in your pussy as I come in your mouth,' Faith stated and crossed her arms over her chest. 'But first I'm going to thrash your arse for failing to obey me in the first place.'

'Please -' Mel whispered again, shaking her head.

'Shut up!' Faith snapped. 'Now stand up or I'll double your punishment.'

Mel slowly got to her feet. Every inch she moved was an inch that she knew she could never take back. She wanted to turn and run from this place, to hide in Natalie's arms and forget all about the young mistress. She wanted to escape from the shadows, from the cries and gasps that echoed all around her. But more than that, and God help her for it, she wanted her cries to join with the others.

'Come here,' Faith ordered.

Mel closed her eyes for an instant before she slowly moved around the table. A flick of her eyes was the only order that Faith gave and Mel turned to lean over the table, her shaking hands sliding to the edge. Faith kicked her legs apart and slid her thigh between Mel's legs. The slave gasped and turned her head but Faith grabbed her hair and forced her head down. 'You forget your place, slave,' Faith hissed. Mel hung her head, staring at the table. The Mistress' hand travelled down Mel's spine, coming to rest on her lower back. Mel shivered as she felt Faith's fingers move round to brush the skin of her stomach, exposed by her loose t-shirt.

'You dress like a man … I like that.' Faith announced as she slowly unfastened the belt around Mel's waist and slipped it from the loops of the black jeans.

Mel shivered with fear and anticipation as Faith's

fingers unfastened the button and lowered the zip. She slid the jeans down her thighs, dragging her panties with them. She pushed them down as far as Mel's knees and then ran her nails up her thighs as she stood up. Her palm rested against Mel's buttock, her fingers tapping against the thin white scars that lined the perfect skin. Mel felt the hand lift from her skin and she tensed with the certain knowledge of what was to follow. The belt landed with a severe snap and Mel yelped, biting her lip to stifle a further cry as the freezing sting turned to a terrible burning throb. The sound of the blow and the feel of it on her flesh was enough for the experienced Mel to know that Faith had folded the belt in half. Another blow fell on her burning buttocks and Mel gave a cry as her shoulders hunched, her knuckles white where she gripped the table. Eight more blows flattened her glowing flesh before a lengthy pause made Mel look over her shoulder. Faith was sitting on the seat behind her and as she looked Faith struck a match and held it to the end of the cigarette between her lips. 'What the fuck are you looking at?' Faith demanded.

Mel quickly hung her head, her glowing buttocks quivering as if fearing another blow.

Faith puffed on the cigarette slowly and Mel could feel her gaze boring into her already burning buttocks. She heard the shift of clothing and gave a stifled gasp as Faith flicked ash at her buttocks. She exhaled smoke, directing it at her pussy. Mel shivered as the hot smoke warmed the moisture at her cunt.

'Maybe I should call the barman to bring a bottle of spirit over,' Faith suddenly announced, making Mel jump, 'You won't believe what I can do with a bottle and I've always wanted to know whether alcohol will burn on human skin. My barman has a huge cock, I'd love to make him fill up every one of your holes. I'd

121

mix his come with tequila and drink it from your pussy. Then you could drink from mine - I love the feel of a slave drinking from my cunt. And while you're drinking I'll shove the bottle into your arse and fuck you hard while I fist your sopping cunt.'

Suddenly Mel threw her head back and screamed as Faith pressed the glowing end of her cigarette against her buttock. A freezing shiver ran up Mel's spine as her scream died to a sob. And then she cried out again as Faith's fingers slid easily into her soaking pussy. Mel tossed her head, her pussy contracting around Faith's fingers.

'Well, well, my little filthy whore, it has been a while since you had a good thrashing.'

Mel bit back another sob as Faith curled her fingers, exploring the soft wetness of her cunt.

'And how long since you had a decent fucking?'

Mel hung her head, desperate to cool the terrible, burning desire at her pussy.

'I said how long?' Faith yelled, pulling her fingers free to slap Mel's buttock, right where she had burned her. 'How long?'

'Too long.' Mel cried.

'Pardon, slave?' Faith demanded, slapping her buttocks again.

'Too long,' the slave cried again. 'Mistress!' Her cry turned to a scream as Faith grabbed the belt and lashed her again. After a torrent of blows Faith suddenly grabbed Mel and spun her over to slam her down on the table. Mel's head hung off the table, her hands reaching back to grab the table legs to support herself. After shedding her lower clothes, Faith walked round to Mel's head and slipped her pussy over her mouth, reaching down to snatch her hair and haul her face up. Mel gagged as her mouth was smothered by Faith's sweet tasting, juicy pussy.

'You know what to fucking do!' Faith yelled and as Mel started to suck at the pussy above her, Faith's hand travelled down towards Mel's cunt. She rubbed the slave's clitoris before plunging four fingers deep into the soaking hole. After just a few moments Mel was feasting hungrily at her Mistress' cunt as her passions rose. Faith groaned, her own lust building quickly as she drilled her fingers into the bucking slave. The Mistress climaxed a few moments later, her juices gushing into Mel's mouth as the slave bucked her hips and then relaxed.

When the shivers of her climax had passed, Faith stepped back from the slave and returned to her clothes. 'Get dressed,' she ordered dismissively. Mel slowly climbed off the table as Faith waved for a fresh drink. The slave dressed silently, tears in her eyes. She looked up at the Mistress - she was so young it was hard to believe. How could she have become so powerful at such a young age? Again she sensed the raw power and couldn't help but wonder at the reservoirs of strength needed to maintain it. She found herself staring into Faith's dark brown eyes and for the briefest of moments Mel sank into them. It was then that Mel realised that those eyes had seen more than she could possibly imagine. No one as young as Faith should carry such a weight of history. But then Faith blinked, perhaps realising that Mel had seen so deeply.

Faith's lips curled into a snarl, 'You had better go, slave.'

Mel swallowed, 'My belt?'

Faith stroked the leather that was lying on the seat beside her. A tiny smile creased her lips, 'I'm going to keep it, as a souvenir.'

'And Claudia?' she whispered.

'I'll find her. You go home to your Natalie - but know this, you'll both be thinking of me now when you fuck each other.'

Mel stifled a guilty sob.

'And do you know why?' Faith didn't wait for an answer. 'Because I can give you both what you can't give each other. You can't be her Mistress, Mel, and she can't be your slave. I know that you have given yourselves to each other so completely, there's nothing left to take. But that makes you lovers and you are slaves only to that. You cannot hurt her and she cannot fuck you and drill into you with complete abandon. In short, you cannot use and abuse each other in the way that you both crave. And when you realise that, Mel, come and find me.'

Mel turned slowly, tears coursing silently down her cheeks as her pussy dribbled with fresh juice caused by Faith's parting words.

PART 2

A NEW MASTER

CHAPTER 2.1:

There was a close, cloying darkness that didn't retreat when she opened her eyes. Her senses rushed back in a torrent and she realised that something was over her head. There was a tightness at her wrists but she couldn't feel beyond that, her arms and hands were numb. A current of air rolled over her and she knew that she was naked. Her fear made her nipples harden and her chest heave. She heard a tiny trickle of water and she tensed instinctively. The water hit her breasts first and she gasped loudly, fighting for breath. She could feel the water rolling down her chest and stomach and a part of her mind realised that she was hanging from her wrists, which explained the numbness in her arms and hands. The freezing water found her stomach, groin, thighs and then her buttocks and back. The water was finally directed at the material over her head and Claudia struggled as the soaking cloth pressed against her mouth and nose. Fighting for breath, she suddenly became light-headed and as her struggles gradually weakened, the hood was snatched from her head. Suddenly she was back in that barn. She could smell the damp straw and the scent of his sweat. It was happening all over again - just as it had so many nights as she slept. A hand gripped her hip and she was turned to face her captors. The barn was suddenly replaced by a cold, windowless room and Claudia found herself wishing that she was back at that barn because she knew, after everything that she had seen these past years, that he had been an amateur. He had played on the edge of the shadows, she doubted that he had even ventured in as far as she had when she had helped Mel to search for Natalie. But now, as she stared at John, she realised that she was in deeper that she had ever been before and this time there was no getting out. But it wasn't the sight of John that caused her gut to twist with fear, it was the sight of Max standing beside him, a look of unadulterated hate in her eyes. If being with Faith had taught Claudia anything, it was that anger and hate were more worthy of fear than any other emotion. John may have been lusting over her prone, naked body but the look in Max's eyes promised so much more. Claudia swallowed, trying to fight back the tears that collected in her eyes.

'What do you want?' she whispered.

John smiled a hungry, sadistic smile before he replied, 'You, my sweet whore, you are to be my new slave.'

Claudia glanced at Max, 'What are you going to do with two slaves?'

John laughed, 'Max is going to help me break you.'

'Shall we get started?' Max asked, speaking for the first time and sounding bored.

He glanced at her, an angry twist to his lips as he replied, 'Are you giving me orders?'

Max fixed him with an unflinching stare that startled Claudia but she didn't respond.

Claudia turned her attention to him, 'Why are you doing this, John? I've done nothing to you.'

He frowned as he laughed, 'I know you're not naive, so please don't act it, you don't want to piss me off.' He approached her slowly, 'And I suggest you start calling me Master.'

'I'll just stick to Kelso.' Max sighed, crossing her arms over her chest.

Kelso glanced over his shoulder, 'Whatever.' he

snarled.

Claudia watched Kelso as he approached, she wanted to be strong, she didn't want to show fear. But she was scared. So scared that her hands were trembling, sending ripples down her arms to make her breasts quiver. Kelso studied the quivering mounds, a smile playing across his lips.

'Bring me those,' he ordered. Claudia saw Max move to her side and she studied the slave's hand as it was held out. Max knew that she was watching and slowly, deliberately, opened her fingers. Claudia bit her lower lip, as much to stop it from quivering as to stop herself from begging with Kelso.

'That's it.' Kelso smiled as he took two clamps from Max's palm, leaving two clamps behind. Reaching forward, he lifted Claudia's breast and snapped the clamp onto her nipple. There was no build up, no anticipation, just the brutal pinching that made her gasp. He let her breast fall and she gave a small cry as the chain hanging from the clamp swung against her ribs. The second clamp was attached to her other nipple and Claudia blinked back tears as Kelso dropped to his knees in front of her. Whistling to himself, he lifted her legs and made her gasp as her arms suddenly took all her weight. He dropped her legs onto his shoulders, adjusting her knees so that her thighs were spread, revealing the smooth inner skin and trimmed pussy beyond. He studied her cunt for several seconds, still whistling to himself.

'You like people looking at your pussy, don't you?' he asked eventually and spread her labia lips to study her inner folds.

Claudia bit her lower lip to stop herself from responding.

'Can we just get on with this?' Max asked tiredly, holding the two last clamps out to Kelso.

'A little eager aren't you?' he smiled. 'Desperate to fuck the whore, eh?'

'No,' Max replied, turning her eyes on Claudia, 'I just can't wait to feel her flesh sink under the cane.' Her eyes stared into Claudia's and for the first time Claudia saw something other than hatred in the slave's eyes, now she saw lust. If anything - she would have preferred the hate.

Claudia yelped loudly as a clamp squeezed shut on one of her labia lips. She gritted her teeth as Kelso shook the clamp, testing its grip on her sensitive flesh. She yelped again, louder this time, as another grip suddenly pinched the inner flesh of her thigh. She felt a weight pulling at her labia and thigh, quickly she realised that a chain linked the two clamps. Claudia gasped and closed her eyes as she felt Kelso grip her other labia lip. The pinch of the clamp hurt no less for knowing that it was coming. Kelso tugged the two chains, smiling at the cry that it drew from her lips. He stood up, still holding the chains in his large fist. 'Now then,' he smiled as he stared into Claudia's eyes. 'How should you address me?'

Claudia desperately wanted to think of some sarcastic retort but the sting of the six clamps seemed to shut her brain down and so she settled for a cold stare and silence. Her silence was split by a cry that tore from her lips as Kelso harshly tugged the chains at her pussy. 'Answer me, whore.'

Claudia stared at him through her tear filled eyes, her trembling lips squeezed tightly together.

His other hand reached up to grab the chains hanging from her nipples and slowly he began to move his hands closer together, dragging her nipples down and her pussy lips up. Claudia whimpered, closing her eyes.

'What will you call me?' Kelso demanded as he continued to stretch her sensitive lips and buds.

'Master,' Claudia whispered and instantly regretted it. It was a tiny word but it carried so much weight and power. That single word was the first step towards her surrender. She knew it. Max knew it. Kelso knew it. And with that first step made, Kelso released the chains and moved in on her, freeing himself quickly from the confines of his trousers and sinking his hard cock into her hot, slick pussy. Claudia knew that she was wet and hated herself for it almost as much as she hated her weakness that had made her call him Master. But her self-loathing was soon forgotten as Max lifted a thin cane to run it along Claudia's cheek.

'Lash her buttocks,' Kelso announced as he held himself deep within her, 'I want her to buck against me.'

'My pleasure,' Max smiled as she moved out of Claudia's sight. Claudia tensed, awaiting the first blow. For the moment Kelso's thick, unwelcome cock was forgotten. Her concern and attention was for that first blow alone. Max sensed her dread-filled anticipation and waited so many terrible seconds before bringing the cane round in a sweeping arc. Claudia cried out as soon as the cane sank into her buttocks before the sting had even seared her nerve endings. She cried out because her pussy had reacted to the dreadful anticipation and was grasping desperately at Kelso's cock. The nerve endings of her pussy responded to the cane long before those beneath the quickly forming welt. The sting of the blow set her buttocks aflame, cooling her pussy's lust. But then Max was lifting the cane again and the anticipation started all over again with the same effects, this time made worse by Kelso's slow withdrawal. This time, when the cane found her flesh, Kelso thrust forward and Claudia's body bucked violently as her pleasure and pain collided in an explosion of sound and sex juice. Kelso timed his thrusts with Max's blows, laughing to himself as Claudia's body jolted over and over, as if a current of electricity were being passed through her.

'She's going to come,' Max announced.

Kelso was startled and stared into Claudia's eyes that were glazed with both pain and pleasure.

'No she isn't,' he responded. 'I want this slut to be kept hot and eager.' He thrust harder, his hand finding the chains at her nipples and dragging them down harshly, cooling her lust as she screamed loudly. Her scream was enough and Kelso growled as he drove into her, lifting her feet off the ground as his cock twitched and exploded come deep into her.

Chapter 2.2:

She was on her knees, her hands cuffed behind her back and her shoulders wrenching painfully where Kelso was tugging on the chain between her wrists as he fucked her. He held the cuffs firmly in his fist, pulling her arms back so that her back arched as his pelvis slammed her bruised buttocks. Her breaths were pained, shallow and hoarse. Sweat ran in rivulets down her face, back and breasts. Her hands were clenched in tight fists, nails digging into her palms. Her hair, drenched with sweat, stuck in tendrils around her face and neck. Claudia suffered his invasion with her eyes squeezed tightly shut, wanting only for him to finish with her and be done. But he showed no apparent interest in finishing and seemed all the more keen to prolong his climactic build up. She could feel his eyes studying the welts that smothered her back and had he turned her he would have seen the similar welts that lined her breasts. Max had continued to beat her long after Kelso had climaxed the previous night. The slave had beat her mercilessly, driving the cane onto the most sensitive areas of her body - not to break her, as Kelso intended - but to cause her the most amount of discomfort possible. The vicious slave's attentions worked, because not only did the harsh lashes cause Claudia intense pain, but the sight of her suffering served to arouse Kelso who fucked her brutally once more before they both left her sobbing on the cold floor. She must have fallen asleep because at some point thereafter one of her tormentors had snapped the handcuffs around her wrists. The first that she had been aware of the metal bands binding her hands was when Kelso appeared and rolled her over, grabbing the short chain between the cuffs and causing her to rear back as he drove into her.

131

She heard him groan and then gasp before his cock suddenly disappeared from within her and hot, seemingly boiling, semen splashed across the ruined skin of her buttocks. He squeezed the last drips from his penis before he grabbed her arms and dragged her towards the wall. He released one of the cuffs so that he could refasten her wrists in front of her and then attached the cuffs to a chain fixed to a link in the wall. He stared down at her curled form, she had pulled her legs up to her chest and now pulled her arms towards her to cover her knees. He grinned at her and then spat on her buttocks before he turned and left.

Claudia had no idea how long she had lain on the freezing floor, the cold seeping deep into her bones. It must have been some time because when she did eventually try to move she felt his dried semen on her buttocks. She sensed someone approach and tried to shrink away, gasping as the rough floor and wall scraped her battered body. She gasped again as a weight fell on her but her gasp turned into a sigh of relief as a blanket covered her shivering body.

'What do you say?' Max demanded.

'Thank you,' Claudia whispered, fearing that if she didn't the blanket would be taken away.

There was a rustle of clothing and Max sat down in front of Claudia. The young slave studied her in silence that same cold stare in her intense eyes.

'Kelso is an animal,' Max announced suddenly, 'He will break you, but his methods are crude and slow. He will beat you until you break but I know that you're strong and his way will take too long. You must be broken before my mistress finds us.'

'And what will happen then?' Claudia whispered. 'What do you think she's going to do to you? You can stop this now. You don't have to be punished by her …

I'll cover for you … I'll -'

'He'll break you,' Max said again, cutting Claudia's words into silence. 'He's brutal and unrefined, but he will do it.' She was thoughtful for a moment, 'He spent time with Harry Nash, I guess Nash made it all look so easy that Kelso didn't really learn a thing.' Max shuffled closer to Claudia. 'Do you know who has the best skills to break a slave?' she asked. 'Another slave.' She sighed wistfully, her eyes distant, 'That's why my mistress is so good at it, she's felt the other side and she knows what it takes to break someone. And it's not just the pain … or the power …' Max's hand slowly moved forward to slide under the blanket, '… there's another equally important ingredient …' her searching hand found Claudia's breast and squeezed the tender, bruised flesh, making the other woman gasp, '… pleasure …'

'Please, don't,' Claudia whispered, her pleas as desperate as when she had begged the slave for mercy as she had beaten her.

A small laugh rolled from Max's throat as her hand travelled down Claudia's stomach to run through the tidy mound of pubic hair.

'Please,' Claudia whispered again, this time through gritted teeth, even as her hips lifted up to greet those searching fingers.

'Please, what?' Max asked, leaning forward so that she could speak quietly and still be heard. 'Please, stop?' She laughed as her fingertips pushed between the folds of Claudia's pussy and the chained woman's thighs slowly opened, inviting Max to explore further. 'You no more want me to stop then you wanted Kelso to stop fucking you earlier.'

The memory of what had gone before, of the state that he had left her in, came flooding back, bringing with it a rush of juice.

133

'That's it,' Max breathed, 'cream for me.'

Claudia wanted to retort angrily but suddenly her pussy was filled with probing fingers and Max was touching her in places that only another woman could. Claudia gave a tiny cry as her mind shut down and her body reacted to the pleasure. She rolled onto her back and raised her hips, urging Max on with a sharp thrust upwards. Max responded by curling her fingers, searching out that innermost spot. She found it easily and Claudia felt her climax pulling at the edges of her senses. It broke over her in a wave of what was more release than actual pleasure. She cried out and then sobbed as the realisation of what had just happened brought her mind back to life. She stared up at Max, the last shreds of pleasure visible in her eyes. The slave gave a small, superior smile and then slowly lifted her hand to her lips. She licked Claudia's juice from her fingers, savouring the look on the other woman's face as much as she savoured the musky taste. Then she stood and left Claudia to suffer the tiny trembles of her post-orgasmic chill.

*

Claudia's eyes snapped open as the door to her cell banged open. Kelso was framed in the doorway as he stared menacingly at the chained Claudia. He stepped slowly inside and set a high-backed chair in the centre of the room. He walked closer to Claudia and stood over her as she tried to shrink under his gaze. She shivered with fearful anticipation of what he had planned. He curled his lips menacingly and then turned and moved back to the chair, straddling it and resting his forearms along the back. He watched her in silence, his eyes squinting angrily. Seconds dragged into minutes before he eventually sat back a little and reached into his pocket.

He withdrew a square tin, which he opened and set on his knee. He then slipped something off the back of the chair which Claudia quickly realised was a broad leather belt. Kelso allowed his eyes to move from Claudia as he reached into the tin. He took something from it and held it up, studying it with dramatic interest. The shiny metal tack glinted in the light, the wicked looking point seeming to glow with a pinprick of light beneath the glare of the bare bulb. Then, with equal dramatic effect, he raised the belt and carefully pushed the tack through the leather. Once it was through he tested the tack by pressing his thumb against the point. Satisfied, he smiled sadistically at Claudia and then retrieved another tack from the tin. He worked in silence, pushing tack after tack through the leather, making a criss-cross pattern with the points on one side and the flat heads on the other. Once in a while he would look up at Claudia, as if to make sure that she was watching. In truth, she couldn't take her eyes off him. There was something horribly fascinating about the way he pushed the pins through the leather, so methodical and terrifyingly sadistic. He worked for perhaps an hour, pushing pins through that belt until he had covered the entire length with the tight criss-cross pattern, leaving a clear section near the buckle.

He looked up her and the look on his face struck Claudia with an awful familiarity. Suddenly something clicked in her head, something that had been niggling her ever since she had first seen him.

Harry Nash.

'You were there that night,' Claudia whispered.

Kelso laid the belt across his thighs and stared at her.

'I saw you,' she said softly, remembering. 'You were the one waiting for Natalie at her flat. I watched you hand her over and take the money. She was begging you not to do it but you … you just handed her over.' Claudia's voice dripped with disgust and contempt. 'And then, I suppose, you drove down to Harry Nash's weekend retreat and enjoyed yourself at the party.'

Kelso smiled wistfully, 'And what a party it was. I spent my time with the most wonderful lady … I was going to keep her afterwards,' his eyes turned dark and angry. 'What a shame for you that she spurned my advances.'

'She must be a smart woman.'

'Not smart, stupid. Stupid because one day I'm gonna make her pay for refusing me.' Kelso suddenly smiled a sadistic grin. 'Which reminds me, someone refused to fuck me in that summerhouse the other day. I think it's time I collected an apology.' He stood up, the glinting belt hanging from his meaty fist. He swung it from side to side and then laid it over the back of the chair before approaching Claudia.

'Please,' she whispered, shrinking as close to the wall as she could get, ignoring the way the wall and floor scratched her bruised body.

Kelso grabbed her hair, hauling her up.

'Don't shy away from me, slut,' spittle flew into her face as he snarled at her. 'You're my slave now, be proud of that.'

Tears leaked from the corners of her eyes as he twisted her hair in his fist before releasing her so that he could unchain her wrists. When she was free he hauled her to her feet and dragged her towards the chair. She struggled against him but he forced her to her knees and grabbed her hair again, yanking her head back.

'Act like the slave you are or suffer the consequences.'

Claudia froze, torn between her desire to fight him and her fear of what he could do to her if she made him angry.

Kelso took her immobility as surrender and lifted her to her feet. He forced her closer to the chair and then pushed her head down. 'Bend forward and grab the chair.'

She swallowed fearfully and then bent from the waist to grip the seat of the chair, the angle lifting her buttocks up towards him. She felt her breath dry in her throat as Kelso slipped the belt from the back of the chair. 'I won't lie to you, this is going to hurt.' He laughed then and Claudia sensed him raising the whip. The leather cut the air with a whine and then the pins bit into the bruised flesh of her buttocks. She cried out. The stinging blow was like a hundred tiny whips all hitting at once. The whip held her flesh for a second before, with a harsh tug, the pins pulled free of her skin. A cold shiver ran up her spine, contrasting with the terrible burn of her buttocks. Another blow, cutting underneath the swell of her buttocks and she screamed loudly as her sensitive flesh succumbed. Again, that tug and stretch of her flesh before the pins came free. Several more blows moved up and down her buttocks and thighs. Beneath the terrible burning, a warm wetness rolled down her skin, sliding between her thighs and slowly creeping towards her pussy lips. Claudia was weeping openly, her head tossing from side to side.

The beating stopped and Claudia sobbed loudly with relief.

'This is fucking amazing,' Kelso laughed, making Claudia yelp as he stroked her bloodied, patterned buttocks. He reached his hand underneath her, his fingers searching out her breasts. When he found her nipple he sniggered and rolled the hard bud between thumb and forefinger. 'Seems you're enjoying it as much as I am. Aren't you a filthy little slut?'

Claudia gritted her teeth and tried to ignore the way

that his harsh words made her pussy contract. Now that the initial discomfort had passed, Claudia was left with that familiar throbbing heat that slowly crept down between her thighs.

'Well, if you're enjoying it that much, seems a shame to stop.'

Before Claudia realised the implication of his words the whip sliced down across her buttocks once more, striking her battered flesh and making her scream loudly.

After just a few more blows, Claudia sank to her knees, unable to hold herself upright any longer. Her head fell onto her arm and she sobbed loudly, 'Please, no more.'

Kelso dragged her away from the chair and laid the whip on the seat, points up.

'Lie over it - tits down,' he ordered.

Claudia stared at the terrible pins and shook her head.

Kelso snarled with fury before grabbing her hair and pulling her up. 'You'll do what I tell you or I'll do it for you.' He forced her down across the chair and she screamed as the pins sank into her breasts. He pushed her down against the pins, hissing through his teeth with fury. 'Defy me again, bitch, go on.'

'I'm ... I'm sorry,' Claudia half cried. 'Please ...'

'Stay there,' he ordered and slowly released her hair. Without him pressing her down the pain lessened but the pins digging into breasts were still like tiny teeth biting her sensitive flesh. She moved slightly and one of the pins dug into her hardened nipple, making her gasp with surprise as the sharp sting sent a shockwave through her body that wasn't entirely due to pain. Kelso kicked her legs apart and she cried out as the movement sent the pins digging further into her flesh. She felt his legs brush her thighs and then the rounded head of his penis pushed between the folds of her pussy.

He slid into her, gasping as her tight but lubricated

hole gripped his cock.

'You're wet,' he said, pleasure deepening his voice.

To hear him say it brought a fresh rush of moisture to her cunt, making her clitoris tingle. She tried to force back the feelings, to somehow halt the tide of her pleasure. She didn't want to take pleasure from what he was doing, she didn't want to be his prisoner, his slave … but she was and, despite herself, the possibilities of her position were overwhelming. He rode her smoothly, sliding into her pussy and causing ripples of pleasure to run up her spine. His fingers ran over her buttocks, smearing the drops of blood around the pinholes that patterned her flesh. He pushed his thumb between her buttocks, searching out the star of her anus. She gasped as she felt him pushing at the tight hole and then his thick digit slid in. He flexed his finger, probing her anus as he continued to fuck her. She could feel his cock sliding against the distension caused by his thumb and, god help her, it felt good. She wanted him to stop as much as she wanted him to continue and that collision of desires drove her quickly to the point of climax. Whether he realised this or not, he was suddenly gone from inside her and she was spilling to the floor. He lifted the belt and sat himself on the chair, resting against the back. He stared down at Claudia as he gently laid the belt across his thighs and then slowly stroked his glistening cock. 'Come here,' he ordered.

Claudia stood and moved so that she was standing over his rigid penis.

Kelso held his cock at the root, angling it away from his body. 'Well?'

Taking a deep breath, Claudia positioned her cunt over his cock and then slowly sank onto him, forcing herself down. She speared herself on him but kept herself hovering over his thighs and the belt. Kelso's hands rested on her shoulders and then, with a violent push, he forced her down, spearing her on both his cock and the pins. Claudia screamed loudly as the points dug into her thighs and buttocks.

'Right, now fuck me, slave.'

Claudia lifted herself up and then let herself drop down again, hoping that if she fucked him right he would climax soon. Any hope that Claudia might have had that Kelso would finish quickly were dashed when the door opened and Max entered. She closed the door behind her and leant her shoulder against the wall. Claudia half glared at her as she continued to ride Kelso's cock.

'Don't finish her too soon, I want to play,' she said.

'Get the strap and we can both have fun.'

Max half smiled and held up a strap of leather.

Kelso grinned at her, 'You know, if you weren't such a bitch, we'd make a perfect couple.'

Max raised an eyebrow, 'And if you weren't such a wanker, well … I still wouldn't want you.'

Kelso's eyes darkened with anger but he didn't respond. Instead he pushed Claudia off him and then bent to lay the belt on the floor. 'Sit,' he commanded, pointing at the belt. She swallowed and then slowly lowered herself onto the pins, gritting her teeth as the points dug into her punished buttocks. Kelso pushed her backwards and she cried out as the movement drove the pins deeper into her flesh. He was on her immediately, pushing his way between her thighs and driving into her soaking cunt. Claudia gasped and arched her back, lifting the belt free of the floor before slamming back down as Kelso thrust into her. Her cry echoed around the room as Kelso lifted his thighs over hers, closing her legs and trapping himself inside her. Over Kelso's shoulder, Claudia saw Max approach and she tensed. The slave glared at her, lust making the anger shine all the more in her eyes. Claudia lost sight of her as she knelt behind him and slipped the leather strap around her knees. She tightened the strap, forcing Claudia's legs together, crushing Kelso's balls between her thighs. He gasped and a shudder ran up his spine. Groaning as he slowly gyrated his hips, he lifted himself up on his arms to allow Max access to Claudia's nipples. Claudia started to protest when she saw the clamps but her words turned into stifled cries as her swollen nipples were crushed by the tight grips. Max tugged experimentally on the chains attached to the clamps before standing up and lowering her trousers. She wore no underwear beneath and once she had stepped from the pool of leather, she stood astride Claudia's head and then slowly, deliberately, lowered herself down. Claudia clamped her lips shut but Max grabbed the chains at her breasts and pulled vicously. Claudia screamed, her breath a rush of hot air against Max's pussy lips.

'That's it,' Max groaned. 'You'll tongue me properly if you know what's good for you.' She tugged the chains again and then released them when she felt the first touch of Claudia's tongue. The slave made no sound but her pussy quivered against Claudia's lips.

'Is she good?' Kelso asked after a few moments.

'Not bad … I've had better,' Max replied and pushed down on Claudia's mouth, making her arch her back as she struggled for air. 'Grip my arse, slut, or suffocate.'

Claudia quickly reached her hands back to grab Max's taut buttocks and the slave lifted herself up a little. Another tug on the chains and Claudia began to tongue the pussy above her in earnest. Kelso continued to gyrate his hips, his groans growing louder and louder. Max made no sound as she fondled her own breasts, rolling her nipples between thumb and forefinger. ,

'Fuck her harder - I want to feel her nails,' she said to

141

Kelso after a few minutes.

Kelso suddenly thrust his hips forward, slamming into Claudia and pushing her down on the points beneath her arse. Then he grabbed the chains and stretched her breasts upwards, making her cry out against Max's cunt lips. Her nails dug into the flesh of Max's buttocks and the slave ground herself onto Claudia's mouth. The tiniest quiver ran through her body but it was her only reaction as she gushed musky juice into Claudia's mouth. The taste of her and the feel of her flesh squeezed beneath her nails was just too much and, as Kelso twitched and exploded inside her, her own orgasm tore through her battered body.

Chapter 2.3:

'And how is my little slave this morning?' Kelso asked as he approached Claudia. She tried not to shrink away from him but as the days wore on it was getting harder to stand up to her fear. It was three days since Kelso had beaten her with the studded whip and over that time he had started to become the embodiment of her fear. Claudia had many fears. She feared Kelso and what he was capable of doing, she feared her failing ability to fight him and she feared that he would break her if no one came to her aid. But as time wore on all of these fears centred on him. But if Kelso was the embodiment of her fear then Max was the embodiment of her desires. At every opportunity, and seemingly without Kelso's knowledge, Max came to Claudia and pleasured her. Somehow the slave was able to bring Claudia to climax even when her buttocks, pussy or arse had been burning from Kelso's attentions - and maybe because of that. The slave's consummate skill turned every pain and sting into a pleasant tingle or throb. Max could remove painful clamps from Claudia's nipples and then gently tease the aching buds so perfectly that any discomfort turned instantly into pleasure. If Claudia had been allowed just a few seconds' respite, a moment in time to step back and take a cold look at what was happening, she would have realised Max's intent and clever manipulation. But she was given no respite, for that in itself, was all part of the torment and manipulation.

And so she looked up at the embodiment of her fear and somehow managed to meet his gaze. She was pleased that she had the strength of will left to face him, all was not lost after all … at least, not yet. Something dropped onto her thigh, making her jump. She looked down at it, trying to identify the familiar outline.

'Pick it up.' Kelso ordered. She did so - realising that the object was a leather bra. As she studied it Kelso set a tin on the floor beside her. 'Open it.' he commanded. Claudia slowly removed he lid and felt the breath catch in her throat. She didn't need to look up to know that Kelso was smiling that horrible, sadistic smile. His shadow slid off her and se looked up, watching him as he retrieved the chair from the corner of the room. He set it a foot in front of her and straddled the seat, resting his arms along the back. 'Get started.' he ordered, staring coldly at her. Claudia swallowed and then slowly reached into the tin to retrieve a tack. Her hand was shaking as she lifted the tack and held the bra up. 'Other way around, you stupid whore.' Kelso snarled as she started to push the tack from the inside of the bra. Still shaking, she slowly turned the bra around so that she could push the tack through the leather. 'That's better.' he sighed angrily, 'I don't want to feel them while I'm fucking you.' Claudia continued to push the tacks through the leather, creating a criss-cross pattern as Kelso instructed. Her hands shook continually, both fear and anticipation making her tremble. There was something darkly erotic about her actions, something disturbingly arousing. She finished the first leather cup and blew softly on her fingertips, looking up at Kelso, perhaps hoping for mercy. She found none and with a flick of his hand he ordered her to continue. Swallowing past the dryness in her throat, Claudia took another tack from the tin and pushed it through. Every tack that she pressed through the bra made her stomach tighten with fearful anticipation because every tack took her closer to the end of her task. Her fingertips were numb by the time she finished and slowly held the bra out to Kelso. He moved to her and took the bra, holding it up to the light so that the pins glinted. 'Stand up.' he ordered. Claudia didn't want to stand but her body moved of its own accord, responding to the command before her mind could stop it. 'Come here, slave.' he spoke quietly, threateningly.

'Please ...' she whispered as she stepped closer.

'Arms out.'

She stretched her arms out in front of her. 'Please, don't.'

'Shut up.' he snapped and slipped the straps over her arms, sliding the bra slowly towards her breasts. She tensed as the leather, and now spiked, cups reached her flesh. He pushed the bra against her breasts, making her gasp. A flicker of lust shone in his eyes as he moved round to stand behind her. He took the two ends of the bra and pulled harshly, crushing and piercing her breasts. She screamed, her hands moving to her breasts as if to tear the bra away but her fingers only hovered over the glinting cups. He turned her round and studied her carefully, reaching up to wipe a tear from her cheek. 'Well now, don't you look pretty?' Claudia gasped as his hands cupped her breasts. 'I think I'll fuck you now.' he announced matter-of-factly, 'And then I'm going to show you off.' He made her turn and hold the back of the chair. 'What did I just say, slave?' he demanded angrily, kicking her feet apart. 'When I say that I'm going to fuck you, I expect you to make yourself ready. I'll have to fuck you hard now so that you don't forget in future.' A few moments later he drove into her and she cried out as her feet were lifted from the floor. His nails dug into her waist, forcing her down onto his spearing cock. It was only a few minutes before he grunted and pulled free of her bruised pussy and a moment later she heard his come hitting the floor. He fastened his fly and then left the cell. When he returned he was carrying a black trench coat and slip on sandals. He put the coat on her, buttoning it all the way, and then made her step into the shoes. He studied her for a moment before combing her hair with his fingers. 'Nice, very nice.' he sighed, 'They're going to like you.'

Claudia swallowed and asked nervously, 'They?'

Kelso smiled his only response was to say, 'We're going out.'

She looked past him towards the door. 'Max?' she asked.

Kelso shook his head, 'This is all my idea. That little whore has got somewhere else to be. She won't be back for a couple of days so I'm going to have fun without her fucking interfering.'

'Where did she go?'

'You know, she never told me and I don't give a fuck so I didn't ask.' he responded as he slipped a pair of handcuffs on her. He then grabbed her by the chain that linked her wrists and pulled her towards the door.

CHAPTER 2.4:

The club was nosier and far more crowded than Faith's backroom club. Somehow that made this place seem all the more foreboding. Kelso had stripped Claudia of her trench coat and sandals when they had entered the club. She was wearing nothing but the studded bra as he led her towards the bar. Claudia was painfully aware of the eyes that studied her as they pushed through the groups of leather-clad revellers. There was something horribly violent about the way the people were dressed and the loud rock music that was playing over the hidden speakers. The atmosphere was brutal and made Claudia want to shrink in on herself. By the time they reached the bar she was shivering with fear. On their way to the bar Kelso had nodded greetings to a number of people but he suddenly laughed out loud when he saw one of the men sitting at the bar. 'Pete!'

The man turned, he was tall and handsome in an aggressive way and he greeted Kelso with a wide smile.

'You decided to come then?' Kelso laughed.

'After what you said, did you really think I would miss it?' he looked at Claudia, 'Is that it?'

Kelso nodded, 'This is it all right.'

Pete approached Claudia, not once looking at her face, he had eyes only for the bra. 'You got more in than I expected.' he announced, running his finger along the pattern of tack heads.

Kelso smiled, 'Not me.'

Pete glanced at him and then a laugh rolled from his throat, 'You made her do it?'

Kelso nodded.

'You're a vicious son-of-a-bitch.'

'That's why you like me.'

Pete's smile was nasty, 'I don't like you. The only

reason they let you through that door tonight was because I told them that you had debts to pay.'

Kelso shrugged, unfazed, 'Well, after tonight, my account will be settled and all debts will be paid.'

'You better hope that she performs then.'

Both Pete and Kelso looked at Claudia as Kelso said, 'She'll perform ... if she knows what's good for her.'

Claudia stared at him but was too nervous to maintain eye contact.

'She's pretty enough. Is she a screamer?'

Kelso shook his head.

'That's a relief, I can't stand screamers.' he grabbed her arm, making her gasp, and dragged her towards the bar. Claudia looked around desperately, hoping to see someone who might help. Hoping to make eye contact with someone, make them realise that she was not here voluntarily. But there was no one to aid her, most were too wrapped up in their own erotic worlds while those that did make eye contact were more intrigued than concerned. She cried out as he thrust her against the bar and her cry drew a lot of interest. People moved back to give Pete and Kelso room and the very act of making space in front of the bar drew even more attention. Soon a sizeable crowd had gathered and the music, which still played, was quieter - someone had turned the volume down. Her arms were hauled out to the sides before cuffs secured her to the bar top. Pete pulled her backwards, stretching her arms and shoulders painfully, making her bend at the waist. He pushed her head down until her forehead rested on the bar, then he kicked her legs apart and his hand suddenly slapped against her pussy lips. She jumped, more out of surprise than pain, her gasp lost behind gritted teeth as his fingers delved between the folds of her cunt lips. He stood with his hand resting on the small of her back as he explored her pussy and arse.

'Quite tight.' Pete announced and then smiled, 'What a shame Steve's not here.' A ripple of laughter ran through the crowd of onlookers, making Claudia look up. Pete stopped laughing and pressed his hand to the back of her head, slamming her forehead back onto the counter. Stunned, Claudia was only able to stay upright because of the cuffs that held her wrists and Pete's exploring hand at her pussy.

'Give me that.' Pete said and there was a moment's respite as Pete's hand moved from her pussy. Claudia jumped again as something cold and hard slid between her cunt lips. It took only a moment to realise that it was the neck of a bottle and then it was sliding into her cunt. 'Grip it, slut.' Pete ordered as she felt the wider section nudging against her outer lips. Claudia did as he ordered, gripping her pelvic muscles and holding onto the cold bottle. She gasped and almost dropped the bottle when she felt another nudging between her buttocks. The distension made it harder to grip the bottle in her cunt and tiny tremors ran across her buttocks with the effort. When the second bottle was fully inserted, Pete apparently stepped back to admire his handiwork. 'Very nice.' he laughed and another ripple of laughter ran through the crowd. The music had stopped completely now and it seemed that everyone had taken an interest in Pete's abuse of her.

Claudia had been in the crowd just before she had rescued Natalie in Algeria and, although she had never said, she had seen everything that they had done to the blonde slave. She realised now how the sheer weight of the onlookers' eyes seemed to increase her discomfort and fear - she pitied Natalie all the more now but she pitied herself just as much.

As the laughter died away there was a click and then a

bright flash followed by a familiar whirring. Claudia knew the sound - a Polaroid camera. There was another flash and then another - each time followed by that familiar whirring. Claudia sensed movement in front of her and surreptitiously looked up. The barman was standing in front of her, his back to her as he reached up to remove pictures from the large mirror behind the bar. Claudia managed to focus her eyes enough to make out some of the images and really wished that she hadn't. The mirror was smothered in Polaroid photographs, each one depicting a man or woman in a frozen tableau of sexual torture. Some of scenes were worse that Claudia's current position, yet she was painfully aware that the night was young. Perhaps sensing her attention, the barman half turned and smiled at her, 'Just making room for you, love.'

Claudia lowered her head as the camera continued to flash.

'How you doing there, slut?'

Kelso's voice came from close to her ear and she looked sideways at him.

'Pete is going to fuck you in a little while and I know that you are eager to please him in anyway he asks. If not, well, I could always let this mob loose on you.' He stood up without bothering to check if she understood him. 'You taken enough pictures, Pete? Cos' I need a piss.' There was enough inflection in his voice for those nearby to realise that Kelso had more than a visit to the toilet in mind.

'Why not just fuck her here?' someone asked.

'Because,' Pete growled, 'I like to do my fucking in private.'

Her hands were released from the cuffs and she was hauled upright. Kelso and Pete grabbed her arms and dragged her through the crowd. Disembodied hands reached out to grab her flesh and hair, smearing sweat over her skin. The crowd thinned gradually until they were able to move easily towards the door marked GENTS. Pete went in first and Claudia heard him say something a moment before two leather clad men exited the bathroom, hastily rearranging their clothing.

'Oy!' Pete yelled after them and reappeared with a young, naked woman held in front of him, 'You forgot something.' He pushed the woman in the back and she stumbled over to her masters who took her away into the shadows.

Kelso dragged Claudia into the bathroom and moved her over to the bank of urinal basins on the right wall. 'Turn around.' he ordered. Claudia did so and didn't resist as Kelso pushed her backwards until she was perched on the curved base of the urinal. He grabbed her hands and hauled her arms over her head, using the handcuffs to fix her wrists to the pipe behind her. Claudia looked at the two men as they approached, not knowing what they had planned. They stood in front of her and unfastened their jean flies, reaching inside to retrieve their pricks. Neither spoke as they pissed, aiming their jets at her breasts, stomach and pussy. Claudia turned her head to the side and grimaced as she felt a warm jet hit her hair. With a couple of sighs, the two men tucked themselves away and then studied Claudia. Kelso was the first to speak. 'So, what's it gonna take to pay my debt?'

Peter rubbed his chin, 'A bit of whipping, then a fist up her pussy and then, after she takes me all the way down her throat, I fuck her arse.'

Kelso shook his head, 'I can't let you fist the whore, I've got other debts to pay and,' he glanced at Pete's large hands, 'I need her in one piece.'

Pete curled his lip, 'Then maybe you should pay your

debt in the usual fucking way, with money.'

Kelso held his hands up, 'Hang on, mate-'

'I'm not your mate.'

'Look, you can fuck her mouth as deep as you like while I screw her pussy. Then I'll stay in her cunt while you fuck her arse.' Kelso smiled, holding his finger up when Pete seemed about to protest, 'And … you can put the slut in your show.'

Pete smiled broadly as he studied Claudia who was staring at him through her drenched hair. He nodded, 'Yeah, ok, we got a deal.' Without waiting for Kelso's agreement, Pete dropped his trousers and pants and shuffled towards Claudia. He was tall enough that his hard prick pushed against Claudia's lips. He put his hands on the back of her head and pushed himself forward, groaning as she swallowed his length. He fucked her mouth slowly, making her gag as he hit the back of her throat again and again. 'Damn, she's pretty good.' Pete announced, 'Kinda makes me wish that you had a bigger debt to pay.'

Kelso leant against the wall beside him, 'I told you, I'm keeping her. I'm sure that we could come to some sort of agreement.'

Pete slowed his movements and glanced sideways at Kelso, 'I thought you were joking.'

Kelso stared at him in silence.

'Well, good luck to you, man, I can see that this one is going to be a handful.'

'I'm breaking her slowly.'

'Yeah? Well I reckon that you need an experienced Master or Mistress to break this one. There's defiance in this whore's eyes.'

'She's just lived the high life too long. All she needs is putting in her place.'

Pete shrugged and pulled free of Claudia's mouth,

leaving her gasping. 'If you say so, mate, best of luck.'

Kelso reached up to release Claudia's wrists from the handcuffs. Grabbing a handful of her hair he pushed her to the floor. 'Hands and knees.' he ordered.

Pete stepped out of his trousers and Kelso shed his lower clothes. Then, with Kelso sliding between her thighs, Pete knelt at her front and lifted her head by grabbing her chin. His fingers dug painfully into her jaw and her mouth fell open. His cock slid in and Claudia retched painfully, giving a muffled cry as Kelso drove into her pussy. Kelso groaned loudly, causing Pete to say, 'Don't come too soon - you promised me DP.'

Kelso waved him off, 'Calm down, I'm just enjoying the moment. Besides, I fucked her before we came out, I've got a way to go yet.'

Pete pushed into her mouth, squeezing his bollocks against her chin. After a few minutes of fucking her mouth he pulled free and said, 'I've gotta come. Roll her over.'

Kelso rolled her over and then lay on his back. 'Climb on.' he ordered.

Claudia wiped a shaking hand across her mouth and then moved to kneel over Kelso's cock. He held his penis at the root, pointing it up towards her cunt. Taking a deep breath, Claudia lowered herself onto his prick. She closed her eyes as the friction made her shiver but then she cried out as Kelso grabbed her breasts and squeezed. She struggled and tried to get him to let go but he just held on and listened to her cries.

'That's enough.' Pete announced, 'I can't get in the bitch if she's moving all over.'

With a sigh, Kelso lowered his hands and held her buttocks, spreading them to allow Pete better access. After spitting on his fingers, Pete lubricated the star of her anus and then spread some on his cock before forcing

153

himself into her tight hole. She gave a tiny cry as she was speared, her cries growing louder as he pushed deeper. When she was royally filled, her head fell forward and she breathed heavily into Kelso's chest. Pete moved slowly, sliding in and out of her tighter passage. 'You like that, slut?' When Claudia didn't answer he slapped her buttock, 'Answer me. You like it, don't you?'

'Yes.' Claudia whispered.

'What?' he slapped her again.

'Yes.' she said, louder.

'You want me to fuck you harder?'

Claudia swallowed, 'Yes.' And she did want him to. She wanted both Pete and Kelso to drive into her, to fuck her until she screamed her release. She thought of her photograph being placed behind the bar and the thought made her pussy contract. She imagined other women being forced across the bar and seeing her photograph. She imagined women getting turned on by seeing the image, by seeing her cunt and arse filled by the two bottles. And then she was suddenly, painfully, aware of the two cocks that filled her holes. In an instant she was on the verge of climax and she gasped her pleasure over Kelso's nipples. He groaned and raised his head, giving a small cry as he ejaculated. Pete pulled free of her and she felt hot come splashing her buttocks. Sobbing with disappointment and unspent lust, Claudia rolled off Kelso and lay on her side. She pulled her knees up to her chest and sobbed as her pussy leaked her juices but left so much unspent.

When the two men had recovered and redressed themselves, Pete lit a cigarette while Kelso hauled Claudia to her feet and made her stand in front of the sinks. He washed her with cold water, splashing her with it or soaking toilet paper to squeeze over her. When he was finished she stood shivering with the cold.

'Here, have a fag.' Pete told him and handed him the packet, 'I'll dry her off.' He grabbed handfuls of paper towels and used the rough sheets to scrub her skin dry. By the time he was finished she no longer shivered with the cold and her skin glowed pink. 'Right.' Pete announced, studying her glowing skin, 'I've gotta go - that crowd will be getting restless for some entertainment.'

Kelso nodded, tossing the remainder of his cigarette into the sink. He waited until Pete had left the bathroom before he slowly approached Claudia. Her chest was heaving and, despite the cold wash, she was still painfully aroused. He realised immediately and a thin smile creased his lips. 'Enjoying yourself?' he asked. She stared at him, her pupils large and bright. His hand moved fast as he grabbed her hair, pulling her sideways to that he could cup her face in his hand. 'You're going to prove that wanker wrong. You're not going to be a handful and you will lose that defiance from your eyes.' She stared coldly at him and his lip curled. He used his palm to slap her face, bringing tears to her eyes. 'That's better.' he snarled, taking her tears as a sign of submission. He let go of her hair and combed her black locks with his fingers to tidy it up. He didn't say another word as he grabbed her wrist and led her out of the bathroom.

The occupants of the club had gathered around a circular, central stage and they all studied Pete intently as he worked at something on the raised platform. As they pressed through the crowd, Claudia realised that he was setting a long metal bar, that was held on supporting poles, about three feet off the ground. It was as Kelso and Claudia got nearer that Pete stood up and turned to face the crowd, circling as he spoke so that he could address everyone. 'I promised you a special show tonight. I promised you the opportunity to make some money. Have I ever disappointed?' he smiled, waving his hands at the comments that exploded from the crowd, 'Yeah, yeah, whatever.' He laughed again, louder than before, 'Well, if you don't want to be disappointed tonight, I shall need some volunteers - five to be exact.'

'Here's one!' Kelso shouted before anyone else answered.

Pete held his hand out as Kelso pushed Claudia towards the stage. 'Anymore?' he called, 'It won't be much of a competition with just one slut.' He made Claudia kneel beside him while he called for further volunteers. After a few minutes Claudia was kneeling with three other women - all of them dressed. She was surprised by her lack of concern about being practically naked and her only item of clothing was drawing more attention than her breasts ever would. It was surprising how other fears overruled any modesty that she might have had. A voice in her mind told her that she was experiencing the survival instincts of a slave. She refused to accept that - she wasn't a slave.

A fifth and final volunteer was propelled towards the stage and Pete hauled her up. Claudia half turned to watch as the woman was made to stand by the metal bar that had been assembled. Pete studied her for less than a second before grabbing the front of her tight fitting blouse and ripping it open. She staggered as he yanked the material down her arms and cast it aside. He then forced her trousers down her legs and pushed her in the back until she stepped out of the pool of clothes. She wore no underwear and Pete slapped her buttock to move her closer to the bar. When she reached it he pushed her head forward, forcing her to bend over. He fastened her ankles to the floor and then her wrists - securing her bent in half over the bar. He slapped her arse again as he walked past to grab the next woman. It took only a few minutes to strip and secure the three other women and then he came for Claudia. As she stood, she could feel Kelso's eyes on her but she didn't bother to search him out, instead she just allowed Pete to bend her over the bar. The metal was cold against her lower stomach and her shoulders pulled painfully once her wrists were secured. With her head hanging down, Claudia couldn't see what happened next but she heard a whine and then something nudged both her pussy and her anus. She heard the other women gasp and she gritted her teeth as the two phalluses were pushed into her holes. Had she been able to see, she would have shuddered at the sight of the second metal bar that now rested against the buttocks of the five women. There was a soft whine and the bar inched backwards, pulled back to stretch a spring at either end. Claudia didn't need to see to know what was going to happen. The bar was held back for a second before it was released and the bar slammed forward, piercing the five women and making them all cry out. The bar moved back and forth, each thrust equal in strength and duration. Claudia realised that the bar was being driven mechanically and there was something grotesque and darkly erotic about being violated by a machine.

'Alright, Ladies and Gentlemen.' Pete suddenly announced, 'Place your bets! Who's gonna come first?' he sniggered as he slapped the first girl's arse, 'Number one? ...' the sound of another slap was followed by, '... number two? ...' the echo of further slaps followed, '... number three? ... number four? ...' Claudia tensed, knowing that she was next. Pete hesitated and then delivered a vicious blow to her right buttock, making the flesh quiver, '... or number five? Don't be shy now, place your bets! Which slut is gonna come first?'

Any arousal that Claudia had felt in the bathroom faded

quickly under the onslaught of the machine and the eyes of the crowd. The invasion of her body was painful, the discomfort increased by the terrible position that she had been forced into. With no lubrication, it was the phallus that rammed her arse that caused her to give small cries each time the bar slammed against the women. She could feel tears filling her eyes as the onslaught continued and her cries became louder. She heard the woman beside her cry loudly and she looked over to see the woman raise her head, her teeth gritted and her eyes tightly closed. The woman gasped and then cried out again, tears rolling from the corners of her eyes.

'Number four!' Pete yelled and Claudia realised that the woman was in the throes of climax. A number of groans and yells echoed from the crowd as the woman's head fell limp. 'Come on then, who's next?' Pete called, 'There's still time to win your money back.'

Claudia shivered as she stared at the trembling woman - something about watching her orgasm unlocked something inside Claudia and suddenly the thrusting phalluses were not as painful. Claudia felt a warmth rolling down her thighs, accompanied by a chill that ran up her spine. It was a familiar feeling and one that she tried to ignore. She concentrated on the bra and that tacks that pierced her breasts. She tried to hold on to the pain but the more she tried the more her pussy awakened to the mechanical thrusts. Suddenly the eyes of the onlookers bored into her and warmed her body with an electric thrill. She cried out as her nipples swelled within the torturous bra - but even that couldn't save her. The arousal that they had left her with suddenly enveloped her again and she was left gasping and sobbing as the machine continued it's relentless invasion. A woman's cry filled her ears and Claudia could almost smell it as the woman further down climaxed. If it was her imagination then it couldn't have been more vivid as a musky scent filled her nostrils. It was all too much and she didn't hear Pete's call, instead she was lost in her own building climax. The machine swung on, each thrust taking her closer. Her buttocks and thighs quivered uncontrollably, the breath froze in her throat and … just … one … more … thrust … the machine slammed into her and Claudia threw her head back to scream as her pussy exploded and juice dribbled down her thighs. She hung limply, her body rocking as the machine worked on. It fucked her over and over, invading her bruised holes and drawing every last ounce of painful pleasure from her battered pussy and arse. And when she had no more to give, the machine drove on, fucking her still and invading her body that had no strength to resist. At some point she climaxed again and then was lost to the mind-numbing, light-draining pleasure.

When they finally released her she slumped to the stage and curled into a quivering ball. At some point Kelso removed the bra and it was perhaps the sight of her bloodied, pinpricked breasts that made him fuck her there and then. She had neither the strength nor will to fight him and the darkness consumed her long before his come filled her swollen, bruised pussy.

CHAPTER 2.5:

Claudia awoke, groaning softly. She half lifted her head and realised that she was still on the stage. The metal bars had been removed, she was the only thing upon the stage. The club was brightly lit and despite the fact that there were no windows, the smell of stale alcohol - and other things - was heavy in the air. She raised her head a little more and stared down the length of her body. She was covered in dried come. She had no idea what had happened after she had passed out under the onslaught of her climax and she perhaps didn't want to know. She lifted herself onto her arms, coughing and retching as her dry throat ached painfully. When the spasms had passed she looked up and saw Pete. He was sitting a few feet from the stage, his feet crossed on the table in front of him. He was smoking a cigarette and watching her through a haze of bluish smoke. There were other people in the club, milling around as they carried out cleaning tasks. None of them paid her any attention. She didn't see Kelso and so turned her attention to Pete. 'I need a wash.' she said, her voice little more than a whisper.

He puffed on the cigarette and studied her in silence for several moments. Eventually he waved towards the toilet and Claudia struggled to her feet. She stumbled and fell to her knees. Pete made no move to come to her aid and he just watched in silence. The nausea and dizziness passed and Claudia found that she could stand. She stumbled off the stage and staggered towards the women's toilet. Once inside she half collapsed against the sink and turned the tap on. After dousing her face with cold water she felt better and stood for a few minutes, gripping the edge of the sink. She was trying to blot out the memories of the night before, trying to erase the memory of her climax in front of all those people. Slowly she reached forward and turned both taps on. Pushing the plug into the bottom, she watched as the sink filled with lukewarm water. Once it was full, she grabbed handfuls of paper towels and soaked them in the sink. There was no soap so she had only the dripping towels, but she scrubbed herself clean, rubbing as hard - if not harder - than when Pete had dried her the previous night. She stood shivering, dripping water onto the floor, and slowly raised her head to look in the mirror. What she saw froze her. She looked pale and drawn, she had lost weight these past few days. Her skin was bruised and marked, her breasts marked worst of all. She hadn't looked like this since ... since ... she forced the memories of what had happed eight years ago to the back of her mind, her misted vision helping by obscuring the view of her battered body. She turned and grabbed more paper towels, rubbing vigorously to dry herself as she cried silently.

She didn't leave the bathroom until she had stopped crying. Pete made no comment about the length of time that she had taken, he just waved her towards his table where a bowl of sliced fruit and some bread had been placed. She walked over, standing by the unoccupied stool.

'You can sit.' he announced and once she had perched on the stool he waved at the food, 'Eat.'

She didn't look at him - she just tucked in. She ate with relish, devouring half the plate before grabbing the glass of water that had been brought. She drank most of the water in several large gulps and then put the glass down to return her attention to her food. She ate slower this time, giving her stomach the chance to deal with the food it had already had. Eventually she looked up at Pete, 'Where's Kelso?'

'You mean your Master?'

Claudia continued to eat without responding.

'He asked me to feed you and then find you somewhere to rest. He wants you rested for tonight.'

Claudia tried to keep the tremor out of her voice as she asked, 'What's happening tonight?'

'Something to do with another debt he's paying off.' He finished his cigarette and stubbed it out, 'Eat your food and then I'll take you to my office.' Claudia looked up sharply, making him laugh. 'Relax, I'm not going to fuck you. There's a sofa where you can sleep.'

'Any chance of a blanket?'

'Sure.' Pete nodded and studied her, 'Kelso must be making more progress with you than I thought.'

'Why?'

'Because you asked for a blanket and not clothes.'

Claudia stared at him, her hand hovering over the plate. She wanted to make some sort of protest but she couldn't form enough coherent thoughts. Instead she hung her head and continued to eat. Pete sniggered and lit himself another cigarette.

When she had finished eating, he led her to his office above the club and left her. She settled on the sofa, pulling the blanket over her naked body and was asleep almost instantly. The day passed quietly and she slept through much of it. She stayed awake long enough to eat some more food that Pete brought her and then settled down again. It was dark when the sound of the door opening woke her. She recognised Kelso's silhouette instantly and felt her fear rise until her blood was pounding in her ears. He made her dress in the trench coat and sandals, thankfully the leather bra was nowhere to be seen. Once the coat was buttoned, he snapped handcuffs around her wrists and led her out of the club.

*

162

The car park level was two below ground and stank of petrol and damp. The lighting was poor, creating vast shadows in every corner. Kelso turned the engine off and told her to wait in the car. She watched him through the windscreen as he approached a large black vehicle. It was hard to tell from this distance but the vehicle looked like a limousine. She watched Kelso climb into the back and her nervousness grew. Whoever owned that car had money and Claudia knew enough about this world of Masters and Slaves to know that money, power and sex were often a bad combination - for the slaves. She sat in the dark car, trying her best to stay calm, experience telling her that the greater her fear, the more sensitive she would be. Minutes dragged by like hours until Kelso eventually exited the car. As she watched, the other doors of the limo opened and all of her best efforts to remain calm were instantly lost as she stared at the three suited men. Kelso approached the car and for the first time Claudia considered her chances of escape. He had left the keys in the ignition, she could just lock the doors and slide across the seat. She looked up to see how close Kelso was and was instantly captured by one of the suited men's gaze. His stare held her immobile for precious moments and, even from this distance, from inside the car, his stare made her skin tingle as if there was electricity in the air. She was freed from his stare by the door opening at her side. She turned to Kelso and her heart sank as she realised that she had lost her chance.

'Get out.' Kelso ordered.

She climbed slowly from the car and stood as he released her hands from the cuffs and then took the trench coat off her. He made her step out of the sandals and then turn around so that he could recuff her wrists behind her back. He took her arm and led her over to the waiting

163

men. The man who stood in the middle, the one who had captured her with his gaze, took a step forward. He was a little over middle-aged, his hair greying at his temples. His face was distinguished and well angled, his eyes were an amazing ice blue that captivated Claudia even more now that she was closer to him.

'Make her kneel.' the man announced, his voice quiet yet sharp.

Kelso pushed on Claudia's shoulder, forcing her to her knees. The man looked sharply at Kelso, apparently angered by the way he carried out the request. 'This is how you treat your slave?' the man asked.

Kelso stared at him in silence.

'Stand up.' he told Claudia.

She looked up at him, confused.

'Do what you're fucking told.' Kelso snarled, grabbing her hair and hauling her to her feet. The man tutted, making Kelso glare at him, 'What is your problem, Rogers?'

He studied Kelso as someone might study a bug. After several moments he turned back to Claudia, his eyes moving down to her breasts. He sighed and slowly shook his head, 'You should not treat such fine breasts like this. These beautiful mounds deserve to wear the lines of an expensive crop. You are too brutal to such beautiful titties.'

'Whatever.' Kelso sighed, 'As long as I'm enjoying myself with her, what does it matter?'

Rogers shook his head, 'It matters a great deal. A slave is a piece of fine marble, to be sculpted and polished. You seem content to brutalise this slave - but you will ruin her beauty and flaw her perfect skin.'

'Look, do you want to fuck her or not?' Kelso demanded.

'No. I want more than that - I want to have her.'

'That wasn't our deal. I told you, she's mine.'

'I have no desire to take her from you. I merely mean that I want her. For just a short while I shall own her and dominate her.'

'Yeah, that was the idea. So, you gonna hurt the bitch or what?'

'You still don't understand. It's not about pleasure or pain - it's about power. You enjoy hurting her - as will I. But I will enjoy having the power to hurt her just as much. And in turn she will enjoy not having the power to stop me. If you want to break this slave, you must understand that.'

'Whatever.' Kelso sighed, bored, and wandered off to watch from the shadows.

Rogers turned his attention on Claudia, 'Listen to me carefully, I want you to know that I expect you to be obedient and I will punish you for disobedience. I'm not saying this in the hope that you will defy me and give me the opportunity to hurt you - I don't need an opportunity, you are my slave and as such I shall do as I please. I tell you this to provide you with the truth of the matter.' He turned and waved to one of the men who brought forward a bottle of clear liquid. He handed the bottle to Rogers and then retreated. 'You will drink this now.'

'What is it?' Claudia asked.

Rogers lowered the bottle. 'Bring me the crop.' He said without taking his eyes off Claudia. When the man appeared with a riding crop, Rogers took it from him and handed him the bottle. Without being asked, the man moved behind Claudia and released her hands from the cuffs. 'Hands on your head.' Rogers ordered as the man returned to the car, taking the bottle and handcuffs with him. Claudia slowly raised her hands to her head as he said, 'I could have my men hold you down while I pour that water down your throat - but that isn't how I do things.' He moved to her side and out of the corner of her eye she saw him raise the crop. She expected the blow to land across her buttock but instead he sliced the crop down so that it caught her at the point were her back met the outward swell of her buttocks. It was a terrible blow that made her cry out and stumble forward. 'Stand up straight.' Rogers ordered. Claudia did so, her fingernails digging into her scalp as she awaited the next blow. The second blow was even harder and drove her, with a cry, to her knees. 'Adrian.' Rogers called. The second man walked over to where Claudia knelt and she gave a sob as she was hauled to her feet. The man turned so that his broad back was to Claudia. 'Hold his shoulders.' Rogers commanded. Crying softly, Claudia lifted her hands to hold his shoulders. As soon as her fingers gripped the material of his jacket, the next blow landed and Claudia cried out as her fingers dug into the man's shoulders. Claudia sobbed as the punishment continued. The blows were truly horrendous and Claudia quickly realised why - these were punishment blows. Blows that land on buttocks, thighs, breasts or most other part of the body can, over time, become arousing. But these blows to the upper swell of her buttocks and lower back could offer no pleasure or arousal. But worse that the terrible blows that lined her skin was the knowledge that whatever Rogers had planned for her, he hadn't even started yet. Rogers delivered ten blows as punishments and then waved Adrian away before beckoning the other man. He took the bottle, which he held out to Claudia, 'You will drink this now.'

She took the bottle from him with shaking hands and gulped the contents. The first gulps were wonderful on her throat that had dried from the beating but then she had her fill and had to force herself to drink the rest, water dribbling down her chin and breasts as she did so.

'Let me know when you feel ready to piss.' Rogers told her as he took the empty bottle. Claudia stared at him with something close to hate in her eyes. He stared back, his own stare blank and expressionless. Eventually he said, 'I do not tolerate eye contact - you have used up all of your chances.'

Claudia slowly lowered her haze. The still fresh lines of the crop on her back were enough, she had no desire to add more.

'Now then.' Rogers announced, 'Let's see how good you are. On your knees.' Claudia sank to her knees. 'Hands behind your back.' She did so, holding her gaze down as Rogers called to Adrian. The man who she had held on to during her punishment now stood facing her and she stared at his hands as he unfastened his trousers. He wore no underwear beneath and she could see his limp penis - which although relaxed, was an impressive size. 'Take him in your mouth.' Rogers ordered.

Claudia hesitated for the briefest of moments before leaning forward and opening her mouth to the stranger. She rolled her tongue, guiding her cock between her lips.

'Very good.' Rogers commented.

Claudia felt something close to satisfaction as she felt Adrian harden in her mouth. She knew that it was a skill to pleasure a man with mouth alone and it was skill that she had learnt well. There was a click and out of the corner of her eyes she saw Rogers start a stopwatch.

'The record is six minutes, thirteen seconds.' he announced, 'Let's see what you can do. Beat the record by at least ten seconds and you will have a reward.'

Claudia began to work, more to get the strangers cock out of her mouth as quickly as possible than any thought of reward making her suck him with vigour. She used every trick she knew. Clenching her lips tight around

167

his rod and then sucking down his length, taking him as deep as she could. She used her teeth gently, teasing and pleasuring by rubbing her teeth along his foreskin and dome of his helmet. She used her tongue with vigour, stroking his cock and pushing at the rolls of skin. He had washed recently and he, thankfully, tasted clean. After a few minutes Claudia allowed herself to become lost in the task and a part of her started to enjoy the challenge. He had grown to a considerable size and the challenge was to cope with his length and girth as much as to make him come within the time. She took him down her throat and even then hadn't taken his entire length. She forced herself to relax and push on. She heard him gasp and quiver - suddenly she realised that no one had ever taken him this deeply. A surge of pride drove her on and she forced herself to relax again as she took his entire length. He gasped again as Claudia held him for as long as she could. When she could hold him no more she slowly drew her lips back along his shaft, rubbing him with her tongue. She felt his cock twitch once, twice and on the third she plunged back down his length. She gagged painfully but forced herself on, knowing that he was close. She managed to swallow most of his length and pulled back a little as she felt his semen gushing down her throat.

'Five minutes, fifty eight seconds.' Rogers announced and slipped the stopwatch back into his pocket, 'Very impressive.'

Claudia gulped the last of his juice as he pulled back and tucked his rapidly deflating cock back into his trousers.

'And now for your reward.' The way Rogers said it made Claudia wonder if the reward was really for her, or for him. 'Turn and walk towards the car.' She did so, stopping when she reached the bumper - she had a horrible feeling that she knew what was coming next. 'Put your hands on the bonnet.' The bonnet was fairly low for her height and, even with her arms straight, her body was bent. 'Hands further forward.' She slid her hands along the polished bonnet until she was bent in half, her buttocks prominent. Adrian opened the rear door and retrieved a bag. The car rocked slightly as he shut the door again and carried the bag over to Rogers. Claudia watched him in the windscreen as Adrian held the bag open. Rogers noticed her looking and snapped, 'Head down.' She quickly hung her head, which served to provide her with an upside-down view of the two men. Her breath caught in her throat when she saw the size of the butt-plug that Rogers retrieved from the bag. It really was huge and moulded out of crimson latex. He approached Claudia, eyeing her buttocks. Slowly he nodded, 'Lubricant, please, Adrian.'

The man brought a tube of KY and quickly squeezed the cold gel between Claudia's buttocks, making her jump. He used his finger to lubricate the outer edge of her anus and then spread a generous amount on the huge butt-plug. Even with the lubricant, it was a struggle for Rogers to insert the plug and by the time it was deeply rooted inside her Claudia was gasping for breath.

'Just relax and breathe normally.' Rogers told her, 'You can handle it.'

She did as he said, allowing her breath to slow so that her body could relax. Her heart rate eased and she found the stretching less painful - it was still a discomfort, but a bearable one. Rogers appeared by her side and she half turned to see what he carried in his hands. He held it up so that she could see it. The paddle was beautifully crafted into the shape of a hand and covered in leather the same crimson as the plug that invaded her anus so tightly. The sight of it made her pussy warm and her nipples harden. There was something beautifully erotic about the paddle that aroused Claudia despite her predicament. Rogers stared at her and she knew, without a doubt, that he would use the paddle harshly and, god help her, she could hardly wait. Rogers perhaps saw the anticipation in her eyes because he reached out to pat her breasts with the paddle. 'I would have loved to paddle your breasts - but with these marks there already ...' he shook his head sadly and moved round to stand just behind her and to the side. 'Your buttocks are almost as perfect as your breasts. They are quivering so beautifully as your pussy reacts to that plug inside you. I know that you are getting aroused, I can see your swollen lips.' His hand ran down the curve of her buttocks and then circled them, bringing the nerve endings to life. 'Brace yourself, I shall beat you now and I want you to cry out only when you can bear to stifle your cries no more.'

The paddle landed with a resonating smack that echoed around the car park. Claudia's shoulders hunched and she gritted her teeth to stop a cry escaping her lips. Another blow and then another. Each blow rocked the butt-plug deep inside her, increasing the discomfort. Soon the warmth of the blows began to radiate outwards, travelling up her spine and down between her thighs, creeping between her legs to warm her pussy. By the time her buttocks were glowing red, Claudia was finding it harder to stifle her cries as the discomfort slowly turned to quite the opposite. A few more blows and Claudia was panting with lust.

Suddenly Adrian pulled the plug from her anus and her cry that she had managed to stifle for so long suddenly tore from her throat. Her anus was left open and the other man was able to slip a set of large anal beads into her with hardly any resistance. Claudia gasped as she was filled with the beads, only the ring poking out from between her buttocks.

'Turn around.' Rogers ordered, 'Sit yourself on the bonnet.' Claudia did so, gasping as her burning buttocks pressed against the cold, smooth metal. 'Feet on the bumper.' She raised her legs and the two men moved in and positioned her feet so that her thighs were spread wide. They secured her ankles with leather cord and then retreated back into the shadows. Rogers moved in between her legs and she closed her eyes as she anticipated his entry. Something cold touched her pussy lips and she gave a cry as gentle vibrations rippled along her clitoris. He rubbed the smooth vibrator between her lips, making her groan with delight. After several strokes he held the phallus against her clitoris, making her quiver. 'Take it.' he ordered. Claudia's hand slowly reached for the vibrator and as soon as she held it she felt an overwhelming desire to plunge it into her pussy. 'Hold it there.' Rogers commanded. Only the memory of the punishment that she had received kept her from plunging the vibrator into her soaking cunt. 'Good.' Rogers said thoughtfully. Claudia had her eyes close, concentrating on fighting her lust, but even without seeing Rogers she knew that he was studying her. She could almost feel his eyes burning her skin.

'You want to fuck yourself, don't you?'

'Yes.' Claudia whispered - she would have preferred not to answer but feared the consequences. Right at that moment she would have preferred Kelso standing over her. He was a vicious, sadistic son-of-a-bitch bit that was all. Rogers was vicious, sadistic and so much more. His power crept along her skin and she sensed that it had the ability to arouse her almost as much as the vibrator at her cunt.

'Who am I?' Rogers asked, 'For this night, who am I?'

She swallowed - wanting to answer this question even less than the first. 'Master.' she whispered.

'Then address me properly when you speak me.' His voice was quiet but with a threatening undercurrent just beneath the surface, 'Do you want to fuck yourself?

'Yes, Master.'

'I bet you do.' he responded, 'So why don't you?'

Claudia's hand quivered. 'Because you haven't told me to ... Master.'

'So, you can show some restraint. Well, you do learn fast. Excellent.' he breathed. Claudia whimpered, the gentle vibration against her clitoris was getting painful. 'What's the matter, slave?'

'Master.' she gasped, her voice quivering as much as her hand, '... I ... I ... need to ... to ... fuck myself ... Master.'

'Yes, you do, don't you?' Rogers replied, 'You really would love to make yourself come, right in front of all of these strange men.'

'Yes, Master.'

'Well, aren't you a filthy little whore?'

Claudia didn't answer.

'Answer me. Tell me what you are and I'll let you fuck yourself.'

'I'm a filthy whore!' Claudia cried, desperate to bring an end to the torturous arousal.

'You certainly are.' he replied and laughed softly, 'Well then, wank away my little slut. Make yourself come. Show us all what a dirty little whore you are.'

Claudia slowly lifted the vibrator from her clitoris and as soon as it was free of her flesh she almost came to her senses. The arousal leaked away as if she had been doused in cold water.

'Well?' Rogers demanded.

'Please ... I ... I ... I can't.' Please don't make me.'

'I'm not making you do anything. You're the one who wants to fuck yourself. So, get on with it.'

She felt his eyes on her, felt the eyes of the two men on her. She was suddenly, painfully, aware of her spread legs and lewd position that she had been tied in. Her pussy was exposed and open, the humming vibrator stirring the air around her cunt lips. Her body quivered and the beads deep on her anus seemed to swell. Her arousal returned like a charge of electricity, humming down her arms and legs, just as she knew the vibrator would feel if she slid it into herself. The very thought of sliding the cold phallus into her cunt, of surrendering, was enough to make her give a cry and push the domed end between her soaking lips. As soon as the humming phallus found her pussy, there was no stopping. She cried out again, louder, and drove the vibrator into her cunt. She had to lift her back off the bonnet to drive it in deeply, her fingers pushing at her lips and clitoris.

'Good' Rogers breathed.

Claudia tried to ignore him but the more she tried the more she felt his stare on her thrusting hand. It was intoxicating and soon she was gasping her pleasure and sliding her buttocks down to meet the thrust of her hand. Despite her incredible arousal, her orgasm built slowly, dragging all her senses and feelings to that single point where her hand thrust the vibrator. She gasped, cried out and then heaved for breath, her tortured breasts rippling. She was on the point of climax when Rogers suddenly grabbed the ring at the end of the anal beads and yanked them free. Claudia screamed loudly, tossing her head and convulsing violently as her climax broke over her in a spray of juices. She was lost on the tide of her pleasure, drowning in the mind numbing, nerve jangling release.

It was a few minutes later that they untied her ankles

and she slid to the cold floor of the car park, too weak to move. Her climax was still singing along the nerve endings of her pussy, making her muscles throb and spasm. She gave a small groan and looked up at Rogers who stood over her, careful not to let her gaze travel higher than his waist. 'Master.' she whispered, 'I need to go to the toilet.'

'And?'

'May I go behind the car, Master?'

He laughed, 'You've just fucked yourself in front of all of us. We've just watched you scream and shudder in climax. And now you want to piss in private?'

She bit back a sob. 'Please, Master.' The need to urinate was almost painful now and she could not, would not, allow herself to piss in front of these men.

'Why do you think I gave you water to drink? I like to watch a slave piss.' Rogers announced with amusement.

Claudia doubted that and believed that the truth was he liked his slaves to beg him to allow them to do even the most basic of functions.

'Please, Master.' she whispered, her stomach and bladder aching painfully, 'Please, may I go behind the car.'

'Very well.' Rogers sighed and waved towards Kelso's car, 'Go over there. I don't want your piss near my car.'

'Thank you, Master.' Claudia said hurriedly as she got to her feet and half ran, half stumbled over to the shadows behind the car.

When she was done, she moved away but remained in the shadows. The stink of her piss, mingling with the musky scent of her sex juice, added a new level to her debasement. She felt a sob rising up her throat as she looked at Rogers and couldn't help but wonder how many more levels of debasement would be forced onto her before this night was out.

'Are you finished, slave?' Rogers called.

'Yes, Master.' she replied.

'Then what are you waiting for - come back here.'

She stared at him and found that she couldn't move. She wanted to shrink back into the shadows and never come out. Perhaps if she stayed here long enough they would forget about her. She couldn't go out there to him - she just couldn't.

Rogers turned so that he was facing her fully, 'And now I will punish you for disobeying me. Come here and take your punishment or I will increase it.'

Claudia sobbed and stepped out from the shadows. Her fear kept her footsteps slow as she fought down the urge to turn and run. Rogers had the crop ready as she approached and she eyed it fearfully. 'Will you be able to stand or shall I call Adrian as before?'

Claudia lowered her head, 'Please, Master, I shall need Adrian.'

He stared at her in silence, his eyes cold. 'Then I shall add five lashes for being so weak. You didn't even try to take the punishment.'

She gave a small cry, 'I'll try, Master, please, I'll stand alone for the punishment.'

'And another five lashes for speaking out of turn.' he announced and motioned for her to turn around. She did so, tears rolling down her cheeks as she raised her hands to Adrian's broad shoulders. She shivered violently, terrified of the punishment that was to follow. The crop fell with terrible accuracy, catching that same area of her lower back as before. The pain was horrendous, making her scream loudly. She managed to take a further eight blows before her legs gave way and she collapsed to her knees.

'Stand up.' Rogers ordered.

'Please, Master, I can't bear anymore.'

175

'Stand up.' he said again, his voice unemotional.

Claudia climbed slowly to her feet and lifted her hands to his shoulders. This time Adrian raised his own hands to hold hers and keep her upright. The punishment continued and after four more blows her legs gave way again but Adrian held her up.

'Weak.' Rogers sighed after he had delivered the final blow, 'I thought you were stronger.'

Adrian released her hands and she sank to the floor.

'Let's hope that you do not disappoint further.' He said nothing more and just turned and walked towards the car. Adrian grabbed Claudia's arm and hauled her to her feet. He dragged her after him and waited until Rogers had climbed into the back before he pushed her inside, closing the door behind her.

The back of the limo was spacious and Claudia knelt on the carpeted floor while Rogers lowered his trousers and pants.

'Straddle me, slave.'

Claudia stood and moved to climb onto his hard prick. Rogers' hand suddenly slapped her thigh. 'Did I say to face me? Why would I want to look at your face while I fuck you?' he slapped her thigh again, 'Now turn around and put your knees either side of me legs.'

It was awkward to manoeuvre in the car but somehow she managed to get her knees on the leather seat. She lowered herself a little and felt his cock nudging at her swollen pussy.

'Take me in, slave.' he ordered and then groaned as she slid down his shaft. When he was buried deep within her he suddenly pushed her in the back, forcing her forward until she was supported on her hands. He held onto her hips, keeping her skewered while he allowed her time to gain her balance. 'Now, ride me, slut.'

Claudia slowly lifted her hips and then let herself fall

back onto him.

'Harder.' he commanded.

She drove herself down onto him, gasping as the angle of penetration skewered her painfully.

'Harder.' he ordered again, using his hands to force her down onto his cock.

She rode him fiercely and he dug his nails into her hips as he forced her down. After a few minutes she was sobbing softly.

'Does it hurt, slave?'

'Yes, Master.' she gasped.

'Does it feel good?'

'Yes, Master.' And God help her it did feel good.

'Are you going to come, slave?'

'If you permit it, Master.'

Rogers laughed, 'You are a fast learner. Very well, if you can come before I do then you are permitted.'

'Thank you, Master … ahhh!' her cry echoed around the car as his thumb slid into her anus. And then she was grinding herself onto his cock and her cries became moans as her climax ripped through her, driving her into near unconsciousness.

She didn't feel Rogers come and only had a vague awareness of him pushing her off. The next time she was fully aware she was lying on her back, on the floor of the limo, with Adrian fucking her mouth while the other man pounded her pussy with his large cock. Rogers was sitting smoking a cigar, once in a while flicking hot ash at her rippling breasts. Before either man had come, she was rolled over and Adrian fucked her arse while the other man wanked in her face. Adrian climaxed with a grunt and pulled free to spray stinging, hot semen across the lines over her lower back. She was still gasping from the sting as the other man sunk into her arse, crushing her beneath him as he collapsed onto her to ride her violently.

At some point after she saw Kelso and was vaguely aware that she was laying on the back seat of his car. He suddenly loomed over her and she felt his cock sliding into her cunt but she had drifted into exhausted unconsciousness long before he climaxed.

Chapter 2.7:

Claudia awoke on the back seat of Kelso's car. She rubbed her eyes and groaned as every tiny movement caused her body to ache. She lay still for a moment, feeling the vibrations of the car as it moved. She had a vague memory of sleeping on rough bedding somewhere - so how had she ended up in the car?

'You awake?' Kelso's voice drifted to her from the front seat, 'That's a fucking relief. I'm sick of carrying you around.'

Claudia contented herself with glaring at the back of his headrest.

'There's food in the foot well. Eat.' he ordered.

Claudia half rolled onto her side so that she could reach the white plastic bag. The more she moved the easier it became and she was able to lift herself up a little. She realised then that she was naked, covered only by a thin blanket. It didn't bother her as much as it would have previously - all that mattered was having something to eat. She opened the bag and retrieved sandwiches and a bottle of water, obviously from a roadside petrol station. She didn't even read the label on the sandwich, just ripped it open and started eating. She had devoured half the sandwich when she asked, 'Where are we going?'

'To see a friend of mine.'

Claudia sighed, 'More debts to pay?'

He gave a small laugh, 'No. This is purely for fun.'

She had no doubt that the fun he was referring to would be for him and not her. The sandwich that she had eaten suddenly felt heavy in her stomach and she put the remainder into the bag. She opened the bottle and downed much of the water in one go, gasping for breath as she lowered the bottle but feeling better once she had regained her breath.

'Eat all the sandwich.' Kelso ordered, 'You'll need to keep your strength up.'

Claudia thought of what had happened the night before - could it get any worse?

It was sometime later that Kelso pulled into a lay-by and turned in the front seat, beckoning Claudia to him. She leant forward and sat still while he first handcuffed her wrists and then tied a blindfold around her eyes.

'Sit back.'

She did so, hoping that the end of their journey wasn't far because the blanket had pooled around her waist, leaving her marked breasts exposed. If Kelso was concerned by her nakedness, he showed no sign. He just started the engine and drove on.

*

Every stumbled, blind step was even more dread-filled than the last. Every step seemed to take an eternity, making it feel as if she had been walking for hours. The darkness heightened all her other senses but with no visual reference it was impossible to determine exactly what her senses were trying to tell her. In the darkness everything seemed larger and more threatening. She felt people watching her and she suddenly had the overwhelming feeling that she was in a large room with hundreds of people watching her. She suddenly had that flash of memory again and she was in the crowd that had watched Natalie being tortured and abused. The memory made her heart thump against her ribs, making her cry out as her hands were suddenly yanked over her head. She had been so lost in fearful thoughts that she hadn't realised that they had stopped. She kicked out, too terrified to submit. She had to fight. A hand slapped her cheek, rocking her head sideways and making her sob. She hung her head, tears soaking into the blindfold as her hands were secured over her head. Her feet barely touched the floor and she swung from side to side, her body turning as she tried to hold herself up. A pair of hands suddenly gripped her hips, steadying her as another hand lifted her breast. She gave a small cry as her nipple was suddenly squeezed within a clamp. Her other nipple was similarly pinched and a cold chain rested against her skin, joining the two clamps together. Fingers pulled at her hair as the blindfold was untied and then lowered from her eyes. She blinked rapidly, her eyes filling with tears as the sudden light blinded her. Her tears gradually dried and the light faded to a more bearable level, revealing a sun-lit room with large open doors on her right. She was reminded of Faith's morning room but this was so much grandeur. The more her vision cleared, the more she could take in her surroundings and she realised that her feet, which barely touched the floor, were not actually touching the floor at all but a dais raised some two feet above the solid oak floor that surrounded her. The circle of her vision grew steadily until, with a shake of her head, she was able to see another dais some twelve feet away. An ornate chair was set on that dais and in that chair, hands resting lightly along the arms, was a middle-aged woman that Claudia feared instantly. Her eyes were the colour of ice - her gaze just as hard and cold. She held all her power in that stare and it was truly terrifying. Faith had a stare like that, when her eyes could have chilled Hell's Fire. Faith's coldness came from her history, from what had been done to her, from what she had done to survive. But the cold stare that froze her now was the stare of a woman who had never suffered, never gone without, and she was clearly someone who could get and do anything that she wanted. She was dressed in black and the jewellery at her neck looked extortionately expensive. Claudia couldn't hold her gaze for long and turned her gaze to the side - there she met another stare that did little to ease her fears. The younger woman kneeling beside the Mistress had darker eyes but her stare was no less cold. She was dressed in nothing but thin strips of leather that circled her throat, crossed her breasts and nipples and dove between her thighs. She was also wearing expensive jewellery - around her wrists and ankles. Claudia had never seen a slave dressed so expensively. As Claudia watched the Mistress lifted her hand and started to stroke the slave's slicked back, jet hair. The slave closed her eyes for an instant, tilting her head slightly to the side. With the gaze broken, Claudia turned her attention to two naked women kneeling on the floor under the dais. They knelt with their heads bowed, hands behind their backs.

'Have you been good, my Colette?'

Claudia looked up as the seated woman spoke and she saw the slave beside her slowly open her eyes.

'I have served you to the best of my ability … and more, Mistress.' she responded.

'And do you deserve a reward?'

Colette pushed her head into her Mistress' palm, 'If you feel that I am worthy, Mistress.'

Her Mistress stroked her face, slowly running her nails down her cheeks, studying Claudia as she did so. Her gaze was like a heat creeping over Claudia's skin. 'Yes,' she said after several moments' silence, 'I think you have been very good.' She slowly reached down to the side of her chair and lifted a thin cane. Colette's eyes widened when she saw the cane being offered and slowly raised her hand to take it.

'Thank you, Mistress.' Colette whispered and slowly climbed off the dais. She approached Claudia, her steps careful and measured. Claudia's eyes shifted to the side, as Kelso appeared to walk towards the other dais.

The Mistress watched him approach. 'Still dressed?' she asked.

'My apologies, Mistress.' he said quickly and started to undress.

Claudia's attention returned to the slave as she climbed onto the dais.

'How many, Mistress?' Colette asked, bending the cane between her hands.

'Until I say stop.' she said as her icy gaze studying Claudia, 'She looks like she can take it.'

'Yes, Mistress. Shall I turn her sideways?'

'No, I want to see her reaction as you whip her.' she replied and then turned her attention to the kneeling slaves, 'Haven't you two whores neglected out guest long enough?'

The two slaves quickly got to their feet and approached the now naked Kelso as he leant back against the dais.

'Shall we begin, slut?'

Claudia looked over her shoulder at the smiling Colette. 'You call me a slut? Have you looked at yourself lately?' As soon as she said it she knew that she shouldn't have. Anger glinted darkly in the slave's eyes and rippled along her arm as she raised the cane. Claudia turned back to stare forward and heard the swish of the cane. It landed a few inches below the welts that lined her lower back, slicing across her buttocks that had been severely bruised by the paddle the night before. Tears sprung instantly into her eyes as a tiny cry escaped her lips. Another blow, the back swing, was harder and lower that the first and Claudia's cry was louder. Through her tear-misted vision she could just make out the shape of one of the slave's sucking Kelso's cock firmly while he pinched and scratched the other slave's breasts. She couldn't see him clearly but she knew that he was watching her. Another blow drew a fresh cry from her lips and she looked over her shoulder at Colette, using her eyes to beg for mercy. She knew that the slave could not stop the beating, but if she could just soften the blows. She tried to convey all this in her eyes but even if she had screamed her plea, Colette wouldn't have heard her. The next blow landed, harder than all the others, and Claudia screamed loudly. She turned back and found her misted gaze fall on the seated Mistress. The older woman was studying her with mild interest. The next set of blows caught Claudia just beneath her buttocks, causing her back to arch. Her feet left the ground for a moment and she was left to fight to regain her footing as her arms were stretched painfully. Her frantic movements sent the clamps at her nipples swinging wildly and she gasped as her breasts were painfully stretched.

'What are the marks on the whore's breasts?' Claudia heard the Mistress asked.

'I made the bra that we talked about,' Kelso replied, his voice deep and throaty, the slave was clearly doing a good job on his cock.

The Mistress leaned forward, 'Whip her breasts for a while, Colette, and let's see how she reacts to some real pain.'

'Please.' Claudia whispered to Colette as she moved round to the front. Finding no sympathy there, she looked at the Mistress and half cried, 'Please … don't … I can't take anymore.'

'It speaks to me?' the Mistress was furious, 'Kelso, explain this!'

'My apologies, Mistress.' Kelso responded quickly, harshly pushing the slaves away. He grabbed something from the dais and moved quickly to Claudia, jumping up to stand in front of her. 'You shouldn't have spoken to the Mistress - she'll make you suffer for that.' The glint in his eyes suggested that he would enjoy every minute and there was a smile on his lips as he pushed the ball gag between her lips. He fastened it tightly and then returned to the waiting slaves.

'How tight are the clamps?' the Mistress asked.

Colette reached up and harshly tugged each clamp before turning back to her Mistress, 'They're secure, Mistress.'

'Take them off with the cane.'

'Yes, Mistress.' Colette breathed excitedly and moved to stand at Claudia's side. She rested the cane on Claudia's breast, just above the nipple. Claudia turned her head away but kept her eyes on the cane as it was slowly raised into the air. It came down with a quick flick, slicing at the clamp and loosening it without dislodging it. Claudia screamed against the gag. It took another four blows before the clamp fell from her swollen nipple. The second clamp was gone after just three blows but there was no relief for the sobbing Claudia as a series of devastating blows fell across her breasts. She tossed her head, tears streaming from her eyes and beads of sweat flying from her hair. After an eternity of blows, the Mistress gave a wave of her hand and Colette stepped back. Claudia sagged with relief but her body suddenly tensed and shuddered as the cane found her buttocks again. Her whole body quivered, her legs gradually giving way as she suffered yet another onslaught.

When the Mistress called the latest beating to a halt, Claudia was barely standing. Her head hung down and the shudders of her body as she wept were the only sign that she was still conscious. Claudia half raised her head when she heard Kelso groan and watched as he pulled free of the slave's mouth and squirted his come over her breasts.

'Lick it off.' he ordered the second slave who had been fondling his bollocks.

'Yes, Master.' she whispered and moved to the slave and started to lick the sticky mounds clean. Her own breasts were red and lined with scratches.

Still naked, Kelso climbed onto the dais and knelt beside the Mistress. He looked up at her, his eyes glinting with spent lust. 'Mistress, shall I have my slave pleasure you?'

She raised her hand and laid it on his shoulder. Slowly she curled her fingers until her nails were digging into his skin. Kelso tensed but didn't pull away. 'Have you forgotten my place?' she demanded, 'What makes you think that I, the third mistress, would let such a low slave anywhere near my pussy? Have the whore pleasure Colette, she's earned a reward.'

'Yes, Mistress.' he said through gritted teeth and then gave a shudder as she released his shoulder. As he approached Claudia she could see the moon-shaped indentations in his skin. The area directly around each was white, the rest red and angry. 'Get her down.' Kelso ordered Colette.

While she released Claudia's wrists, Kelso moved to the corner of the room. As soon as her hands were free, Claudia slumped to the ground, her body quivering.

'Get up.' Kelso ordered and when Claudia struggled to stand Colette grabbed her arm and hauled her up. She stood for a moment before she collapsed to her knees. 'For fuck's sake.' Kelso growled as he knelt in front of her. He slipped a belt around her waist, sliding it down so that it rested on her hips. Claudia quivered as the leather strap pressed into her welt smothered back. Kelso tightened the belt harshly, making Claudia cry against the gag. 'Shut the fuck up.' he snarled and then buckled the belt before moving back. 'Lie down.' For a moment Claudia thought that he meant her but then Colette moved round and lay in front of Claudia, her legs spread.

186

'Well?' Colette demanded.

Claudia looked down and saw the dildo for the first time. It was black and huge, moulded with veins and a large helmet. Claudia had never fucked another woman like this before and she found it difficult to position the fake cock at Colette's wet entrance.

'What the fuck are you doing?' Colette snapped and half sat up to position the dildo. 'Now, slide it in.'

Claudia pushed forward with her hips, sinking down between Colette's legs. The slave groaned loudly, tipping her head back as the huge dildo filled her cunt.

'That's fucking right!' Colette half cried when the dildo was buried deep inside her. She pushed her hips up, grinding herself against the root of the phallus. 'Fuck me then, you stupid slut.' Claudia slowly withdrew the dildo, inch by inch, making Colette quiver with annoyance. 'No, you stupid whore, fuck me!' Her fingers found Claudia's swollen nipples and she gripped them, yanking her breasts down and making Claudia fall onto her, the movement drove the dildo deep. 'That's it!' Colette screamed, 'Fuck me like that!' She released Claudia's nipples so that she could lift herself up. She hesitated a moment and then slammed back into the waiting cunt. Colette screamed with pleasure, pressing her feet into the floor and shoving her hips upwards to meet the next downward thrust. 'Oh fuck, yeah!' Colette cried, thrusting her hips up over and over, timing herself with Claudia's thrusts. 'Faster!' she cried, 'Fucking faster!' Her hands slapped at Claudia's breasts, sending the mounds swinging as she fucked her as fast and as hard as she could. Suddenly Colette cried out and wrapped her legs around Claudia's lower back, pulling her down and into her cunt. Claudia screamed as her tortured back was crushed beneath the slave's calves. Colette climaxed nosily, tossing her head from side to

187

side. She had barely finished shuddering when Kelso's voice came from behind Claudia. 'Keep hold of her.' he ordered and suddenly Claudia felt something cold and wet being rubbed around her anus. She had a moment to realise that it was lubricant before his cock suddenly drove between her buttocks. She struggled against Colette's vice-like thighs but there was no escape from Kelso's invading cock. He slammed into her, grunting as he held her shoulders tightly. The movements awakened Colette's lust once more and soon she was gasping and crying for him to fuck Claudia harder. He obliged, skewering her harshly and digging his nails into her shoulders. Suddenly Claudia felt Colette's warm juice splashing across her thighs and the sheer eroticism of everything that had happened was just too much. With a shameful, disgusted grunt, Claudia collapsed onto Colette as she was rocked by her own mind-numbing orgasm.

*

Claudia had no idea how she was managing to stand - but she was. After another noisy climax from Colette, Kelso had taken Claudia to a bedroom where he had allowed her to sleep. She had been awoken some time later by a brutish woman who had ordered her to follow. Kelso had been nowhere around and the woman was insistent, tapping Claudia's bruised nipples when she hesitated. She was led downstairs and into a large dining room where she was made to stand with a group of naked slaves. Over the next few minutes further slaves were brought and then they were all forced to stand in line. The brutish woman reappeared with a man who was dressed as a butler. With her eyes straight ahead, she couldn't see what was happening as they moved down the line. When they reached her the man studied her breasts and then made her turn round. He prodded her buttocks and then made her turn back round. He waved his hand and then moved on to the next one. While he was expecting the next slaves the woman snapped leather bands around her neck and wrists. Once those that he decided were adorned with leather straps, all the slaves were told to line up along the wall. Claudia had no idea why about a third of the gathered slaves had been given the leather to wear and there was no opportunity to ask. Things became apparent, however, when a group of well-dressed diners appeared and were seated around the large table. With a click of his fingers, the butler beckoned the leather-clad slaves and Claudia joined them. Their purpose became clear when Claudia noticed the more experienced slaves immediately approach the table and start to pour wine. Claudia helped to serve the starter, a rich coloured soup that smelt wonderful. As she served she glanced at the naked slaves who now knelt with their heads bowed and hands behind their backs. She turned from them, concentrating on serving, fearing that if she made a mistake a punishment would quickly follow. She had seen the butler moving around the table and caught a quick glimpse of a whip hanging from his waist. One of the men at the table declined a starter and beckoned to the butler who bent to listen to his request before nodding and approaching the naked slaves. He selected one, apparently at random, and marched her back to the table. Claudia had finished her serving duties and now, standing back from the table, she was able to watch as the man studied the slave that was brought. He waved his hand nonchalantly and the butler forced the slave to open her mouth. As she did so Claudia caught a glint of metal and realised that the slave had her tongue pierced. Nodding, as someone might accept a bottle of wine that had been offered, the man turned to speak to his female companion as the butler forced the slave beneath the table.

If Claudia thought that being selected to serve the twenty or so diners would save her from any unwanted attention, then she was to be disappointed. It was as she was serving the green vegetables to accompany the main course that another of the well-dressed men ran his hand up the back of her thigh. She finished serving him and stood, unsure what to do next because his hand was still on her leg. She looked across the table and saw Kelso who, with just a stare, commanded her to stay where she was. She longed to hurl the bowl of vegetables at him but that idea and her anger faded under the weight of her enforced slavery. There was nothing she could do to stop the strange man's fingers from pushing between her thighs, nothing she could do to stop him searching out her pussy lips. The very fact that she stood, submissively allowing him to explore her, meant that when his searching fingers reached her cunt, he found it moist. She hated herself for it but was relieved that, if he noticed, he showed no reaction. She looked up at Kelso again and found him smiling - he knew that she was wet and he was enjoying it. She tried to force anger into her eyes but it was getting harder to do. Suddenly Claudia yelped and almost dropped the bowl of vegetables. The man who had been searching out her pussy had lifted one of the serving spoons and pressed the hot metal against her buttock. The butler heard her exclamation and glared at her, his hand going to the whip at his side. She stepped back quickly, taking the spoon from the man and then moved on to serve the next person. The stranger raised his glass in a toast, smiling at Kelso who responded with a laugh.

While the diners ate, Claudia stood with the other slaves and silently watched them eat. It was as she was standing there that the butler approached.

'When they finish their main course, make sure that you take Master Duvall's plate and then serve him his dessert.' Without waiting for her to respond he turned and walked away. He hadn't told her who Master Duvall was and he didn't need to - at least now she could give a name to the man who had explored her pussy with hungry fingers. She watched him while he ate, studying the smooth line of his jaw. He was past middle age and had moved into a distinguished look that kept a young glint in his eye. He moved and interacted with the other diners with an ease that showed his absolute confidence in his surroundings. Claudia studied the other diners and found that confidence radiating from all of them - even Kelso seemed at home and he had never had this kind of power. It was a confidence that Claudia had come across before - the confidence born of finding your place, your standing and nowing that everyone around you knew too. No questions. No debate. Just an acceptance of the way things were. They were the Masters and the Mistresses - Claudia and the other naked women were the slaves. No questions. No debate. No defiance. She looked at the woman beside her and sensed the same resignation from her that she felt herself.

When they finished their main course, Claudia approached the table, realising that none of the other slaves went to Duvall - clearly they had heard the butler's command as well. She was a few feet from the table when he noticed her and smiled. He didn't move until she reached over to take his plate and then his fingers found her nipple. He squeezed the bud tightly between thumb and forefinger. Claudia hissed with pain, her nipples had suffered greatly over the past few days and she didn't know how much more she could stand. He didn't speak, he just sat and held her bruised nipple.

'With your permission, Master ...' Claudia said quietly, '... may I take your plate?'

'I'm not stopping you,' Duvall responded.

Gritting her teeth, Claudia pulled back. His fingers kept a tight grip, stretching her nipple and breast painfully, until the bud slipped free of his fingers. When she brought him his dessert he made her kneel beside his chair. 'But, Master,' Claudia whispered, her fingers stroking the leather band at her throat. 'I am to serve tonight.'

'Tonight and every night,' he laughed and smiled at Kelso across the table. He turned back to her and ripped the collar from her neck and the bands from her wrists. 'There, is that better?' He pushed the bowl containing his dessert to the side and slid his chair back. 'Stand up.'

Claudia slowly stood, looking round for the butler, hoping that Master Duvall had broken some sort of etiquette by removing the leather bands. She caught sight of him for an instant but he was lost from view as she was roughly pushed over the table. She rested on her forearms and looked over her shoulder at Duvall. He caught her eye and a stinging slap landed on her buttock. 'What are you looking at, slave?'

She swallowed, 'I'm sorry, Master.'

Another slap seemed to set her skin aflame and she gave a tiny cry.

'That's better.' He pushed her buttocks apart, running his thumb over the tight star of her anus. She jumped as something warm ran between her buttocks to drip between her pussy lips and down her thighs. She half turned in time to see Duvall raise the empty red wine bottle. He slid it first into her pussy and then into her arse, making her squirm as the smooth glass penetrated her. Once he had pulled the bottle free he forced his

192

mouth between her cheeks and licked her pussy and arse clean, delving his tongue into both holes and making her quiver with delight.

'My, my, you are a filthy slut, aren't you?' Duvall said as he sat back and wiped his mouth. He ran his fingers idly over her pussy lips and turned to the woman beside him and asked loudly, 'So, what would be the quickest what to make this slut come?' A shiver ran up Claudia's spine as all eyes around the table fell on her. Duvall glanced around at his fellow diners. 'Any suggestions?'

The woman beside him was the first to respond, 'A good fucking with that bottle should do it.'

'Pussy or arse?' Duvall asked.

'Pussy,' she replied.

'No,' a man announced from further down the table. 'That whore would want it up the arse, no doubt.'

'Not a bottle though,' someone else said and then suddenly everyone had something to say.

'No, not a bottle … a good fingering maybe.'

'She'd love a fisting, I'd put money on it.'

'I disagree. The slut wants meat. Only a cock would satisfy a slut like that.'

'But she would want to be hurt as well.'

'So, clamp her tits.'

'More than that.'

'Clamp her cunt lips?'

'And clitoris.'

'A good whipping, that's what she wants.'

'While she's being fucked?'

'Of course.'

'She could straddle Duvall and have her tits whipped, she'd come in two minutes flat.'

'If you want her to come that fast she'll want something up the arse.'

'Here you go!' a man stood up and grabbed something

off a large fruit bowl, which he tossed towards Claudia. The banana landed with a thump and the diners all laughed. Claudia looked round and only realised then that she had been silently crying.

'Put it in her pussy!' someone laughed.

'I thought it was for her arse.'

'Just shove it in her cunt, let's see how wet the slut is.'

Claudia closed her eyes as Duvall reached for the fruit. There was a pause and then she felt the fleshy fruit pressing at her cunt lips. She grimaced as a sob escaped her lips.

'Fuck me!' Duvall exclaimed as he pulled the fruit from her cunt. He held the glistening banana up so that everyone could see it.

'Bananas and cream!' someone laughed and the diners laughed again.

Still laughing, Duvall held the banana out to Claudia. 'Eat it,' he commanded.

Claudia took the fruit with a shaking hand and raised it to her lips.

'Suck it first,' a woman called.

'Yeah, make the whore suck it like a cock. Let's see what she can do.'

'You heard them,' Duvall announced and slapped her buttock.

Claudia bit back another sob and then slowly slid her mouth down the length of the banana.

'Go on, suck it!'

'Yeah, suck it, slut!'

The cries rang around her, slashing at her like a hundred whips. She continued to cry as she sucked the fruit, her tears rolling down her cheeks and hands.

'That's enough for me,' Duvall suddenly announced and grabbed her hips, pulling her into his lap. Claudia screamed as she was cruelly speared. He fucked her harshly, his hands finding her breasts and pinching her nipples. Claudia felt all their eyes on her and realised that they were all anticipating her climax. She tried to hold off, to not give them the satisfaction. But Duvall's harsh penetration and deep fucking was just too much. She felt her pleasure rise and when it was on the verge of breaking, Duvall pulled free and splashed come across her back.

Delirious with unspent lust, Claudia knew little of what happened next. Everything became a blur of images and cries. Somehow she ended up lying on a bed with one wrist chained to a thick wooden post. Kelso was fucking her mouth, forcing himself as deep as he could. His bollocks slapped her chin, his thighs crushing her shoulders. When he came he pulled free to smother her breasts and then climbed off the bed. A few moments later something landed on the bed and Claudia jumped as the humming phallus rolled against her thigh.

'You know what you want to do, you filthy bitch,' Kelso announced and then walked towards the bathroom.

Claudia didn't want to, she didn't want to succumb to her lust - but her hand grabbed the vibrator and she wept loudly as she slowly moved her legs apart.

The vibrator was still lying next to her when she awoke the next morning with both her hands chained to the wooden post and Kelso hammering his cock into her bruised pussy. She groaned beneath his violent thrusts, feeling her body stir despite her mind's attempt to override it. Kelso grunted and his cock twitched inside her. His weight fell heavily on her chest as he panted into her neck. Still lying over her, he reached over and released her wrists. Then he sighed and climbed off.

'Shower,' he ordered as he walked towards the bathroom. Moving stiffly, Claudia climbed off the bed and followed him. A few minutes later she was kneeling in the shower, washing his cock clean of her juices.

'I hope you enjoyed yourself here - we'll be back soon enough.'

'What is this place?' she asked without looking up.

'We just call it The Slave House. Your friend, Faith, was one of the founding partners. Her, Harry Nash and a couple of others. I love it here and you were my ticket in.'

'Me?'

'Yeah. I've only ever come as a guest before but now I'm a Master and now that I bring my own slave, all the privileges of the house are mine.'

Claudia looked up at him, 'And what happens when I tire of playing slave?'

Kelso's smile was full of humour, 'Have you forgotten the Third Mistress already?' he laughed, knowing full well that she hadn't. 'Well, she's not nearly as sadistic as some of the others. So, please, the next time we come, play up, disobey me - I'd love to see what the Second Mistress would do to you.'

Claudia swallowed, 'What about the First Mistress?'

He shrugged, 'I've never met her.' He looked down, saw that he was clean and pushed past Claudia to step out of the shower. 'Get washed and dressed. We're leaving in half an hour.'

Exactly half an hour later Claudia was led, my means of a collar and chain, out of the house. Thankfully Kelso had given her clothes to put on and it was a relief to feel cloth on her skin again. It was as she approached the car that she caught sight of a group of slaves exercising on the vast lawn. Her attention was drawn instantly to a young slave who she recognised instantly. 'Phoebe?' she whispered and then, 'Phoebe!'

The slave turned at the sound of her name and

screamed Claudia's name in response.

'What the fuck?' Kelso demanded and bundled Claudia into the car. She fought against him but he was too strong and he pinned her on the back seat. 'Do you want me to take you back inside?'

Claudia relaxed underneath him, tears pooling in her eyes. Kelso climbed off her and out of the car, slamming the door shut behind him. Claudia sat up quickly in time to see Phoebe being dragged into the house. She disappeared as Kelso climbed into the driver's seat and started the engine. Once they were away from the house, Claudia let out a stifled sob and collapsed onto the seat. She cried silently until she eventually drifted off to sleep.

CHAPTER 2.8:

Claudia's legs gave way underneath her and she stumbled into the cell, collapsing in an untidy heap.

'Where the fuck have you been?'

Claudia managed to find the strength to raise her head and was stunned to see Max sitting in the centre of the room. It wasn't the sight of Max sitting astride the high-backed chair, her hands on her knees, that surprised Claudia but the look of sheer fury that darkened her deep brown eyes.

'We went to a club,' Kelso replied nonchalantly as he stepped into the room and kicked the door closed with his heel, 'What's it to you?'

'What's it to me?' Max whispered dangerously, her fingers digging into her legs until her knuckles went white, 'You've been gone three fucking days!'

'Don't tell me you were worried for my welfare,' Kelso sniggered. 'We were just having fun.'

'Are you out of your tiny fucking mind? One of the most powerful and feared Mistresses in the country is, no doubt, looking for us right now and you take the whore on a fucking trip? You fucking idiot!'

Kelso moved slowly to the chair where Mel was sitting. The two of them locked stares for an age before suddenly, and with remarkable speed and strength, Kelso delivered a vicious backhand to the right side of Max's face. The slave was knocked sideways, the chair toppling with her as she fell. Snarling with fury, Kelso grabbed a handful of her hair and yanked her head up to deliver several blows to either cheek before dropping the stunned slave. He turned and walked quickly to Claudia who tried to shrink from his anger. He gripped her hands, wrenching her arms up and releasing the handcuffs. Dropping her arms, he turned his back on her and approached Max once more. The young slave was trying to raise herself off the floor but Kelso pushed her back down and rolled her onto her front before snapping the cuffs around her wrists, binding them behind her back. He hauled her to her feet and pushed her roughly against the wall. She didn't struggle, she just stood there as he tore the clothes from her body. When she was naked he grabbed her shoulder and threw her to the floor. He then grabbed Max's waist, hauling her up so that she was resting on all fours. He pushed her head down between her arms and forced her to straighten her thighs, slanting her back and making her buttocks prominent.

'You're not my master, Kelso,' Max announced, half turning her head - but that was the only movement she made.

'I don't want to be your master - I'm just going to remind you to show me the respect that I deserve.' He slowly uncurled the leather belt that he had made all the more vicious by the addition of the tacks. Max looked at the glinting whip but her eyes showed no emotion. 'You see, I decided long ago that I wasn't going to give you back to Faith. I did consider ransoming you back to her but then I realised that I could get so much more for you. I was going to wait a little longer but you just couldn't keep your mouth shut, could you? Well, now I want you to make some noise. I want you to do something that I've never heard you do …' he paused as he raised the belt, '… I want you to scream.' He brought the belt crashing down across the upper curve of her buttocks with enough force to drive the tacks into her skin and send violent shudders down her thighs and back. He yanked the belt clear, pinpricks of blood appearing instantly to form a criss-cross pattern over her skin. He held the belt by his side and stared at Max - she hadn't made a sound. Claudia also stared at the slave, her eyes wide with fascination - how could she have not cried out? Claudia jumped as the belt found its mark again … and again. Ten or more blows landed on the silent slave's buttocks but her only reaction was an increase in the speed of her breathing. Claudia wasn't sure if that was through pain or pleasure - it was impossible to tell. Kelso was breathing as heavily as Max and Claudia realised that he had been beating the slave more harshly than he had ever beaten her. He struck the slave several more times before his lust overrode his anger and he threw the belt to one side. Releasing his rigid cock, he fell to his knees between Max's legs and drove himself into her pussy. He laughed as he sank deeper into her, 'You're tight - I guess you didn't enjoy that as much as I thought.' He laughed again before digging his nails into her hips. Max's only reaction was to tighten the muscles across her shoulders. She kept her head bowed her eyes hidden behind a curtain of raven hair. He fucked her violently, bruising her cunt and thighs as he slammed into her over and over again. He suddenly gave a small cry and pulled free to shoot his come over the bloodied pinpricks that smothered her buttocks. He squeezed the last drips from his cock and then smeared his come over her wounded cheeks, mixing his pleasure with her pain. With his fingers moist, he suddenly drove three fingers between her buttocks to spear her anus. Max lifted her head, her hair falling from around her face and revealed her tightly closed eyes. Her mouth was slightly open but no sound escaped her lips as her body shuddered with climax. Tiny quivers rippled her body even after Kelso had pulled his fingers free. He stood and rearranged his trousers before picking up the belt again.

'Roll over.' he ordered.

Max did as he commanded, showing no reaction as her tortured buttocks were squashed beneath her.

Kelso stood over her, carefully tracing the end of the leather belt around the flattened mounds of her breasts. 'So, are you ready to scream for me now?'

Max stared at him in silence. She continued to watch him as he raised the belt over her breasts. She didn't even close her eyes when the belt came slicing down across her hardened nipples.

Kelso dumped a bucket of water in front of Claudia and nodded towards the unconscious Max. 'Clean her up,' he ordered. 'I might have a buyer coming round to see her.'

'A buyer?' Claudia asked incredulously. 'I thought you needed her to help you break me.'

Kelso's lip curled dangerously, 'There's more than one way to skin a cat.' He stared at her for a moment and then turned and headed out of the cell.

With a sigh, Claudia forced her aching body to move. She was tempted to use the water on herself, although it would take more than water to make her feel clean. With another sigh she moved painfully towards the naked slave. As she started to wash Max with the rough sponge, she couldn't help but wonder how many more slaves she would clean up. Mel, Natalie, Phoebe and now Max. She thought of Phoebe and the fear in the young slave's eyes when she had seen her at the Slave House. How the hell had she got there? Claudia would have to check it out. That thought stopped her and she stared around the dimly lit room that had become her cell. She stared down at her battered, naked body and felt a sob thicken in her throat. The person who needed saving right now was her. She wiped the back of her hand across her eyes and shook her head. Is this really where her search for Faith had brought her? Is this where her crusade, as Faith had called it, had led her? And where would it lead from here? She felt tears welling in her eyes as fear gripped her chest. She thought about the previous few days. So much of it was a blur but some of it was all too clear. And clearer than anything else were the memories of her numerous orgasms. She shook her head as if she could somehow shake the memories loose but she knew, perhaps better than anyone, that such memories could not be dislodged so easily. Had she been able, she would have dislodged her memories of Faith. Maybe then she would have been able to get on with her life. It was impossible to say where her life would have led if she had just let Faith go. A part of her couldn't help but believe that Faith's world would have found her eventually - after all, she could no longer deny the allure of that world. Where, if she had allowed herself to explore fully, would she be now? Even with all her precious choices intact, would she even now be a slave in training and happily submissive? Had her desire for choice prolonged the inevitable draw of her desires? Claudia bit back her sob and pressed a palm to her temple. There were just too many connotations and routes for her tired mind to follow. She would be driven mad if she tried to second-guess every twist of fate that had punctuated her life. A part of her wished for the attentions of Kelso or even Rogers. At least when she had been swept up with them her mind had not considered anything but her survival through submission.

Max, who gave the tiniest of whimpers as she rolled onto her side, saved her from any further thoughts. It was perhaps the sound of her own pain that awakened her. Her dark eyes snapped open - as if expecting an instant punishment for her digression.

'It's all right,' Claudia said softly. 'I'm not going to hurt you.'

Max's dark eyes turned on her, glinting with hate. 'How could you possible hurt me?' she snarled and, despite the pain that she must have felt, she sat up and dragged herself towards the wall.

Claudia wanted to turn her back on the slave and ignore her but she needed an ally and Max was all she had. Despite her burning desire to just leave Max to her fate, she was smart enough to know that they needed each other. She spent several minutes trying to think of something to say and eventually asked, 'What's it like to be a slave?'

Max looked up slowly, her eyes confused rather than the usual angry.

'I'd thought I'd ask so that I know what to expect.'

The tiniest of smiles creased Max's lips, 'So, you're weakening then?'

'Maybe.' She studied Max as she considered her next words, 'Although I'm sure that Kelso will have a harder time turning me into his slave without your help.'

Max stared at Claudia in silence, her eyes flickering as something worked away in her mind. She had obviously realised that Claudia was doing more than just making conversation. She stared at her and clearly decided to play along to see where the game was leading. 'It's liberating … being a slave.' she announced. 'No one has ever made me feel as special as my Mistress does.'

Claudia could understand and relate to that - she remembered how special Faith had made her feel, both in the past and all the more recently.

Max perhaps saw the look in Claudia's eyes because her tone was angry when she said, 'My Mistress wastes her time with you - you could never serve her as I do.'

'I never wanted to serve her.'

'Then you're a fool.'

Claudia sighed but didn't respond.

'I serve my Mistress with my life, no one else will ever serve her as I do,' Max announced. 'I've seen to that, haven't I?'

'And what would you have done if Faith had brought Natalie home?'

Max laughed harshly, 'Do you think I prepared all this

with Kelso just for your fucking benefit?' her eyes tightened with anger. 'I've been manipulating that dumb shit for months. You wouldn't believe the things I've done recently to groom Kelso for this - and when he was beating me, screwing me, abusing me, the whole time I was whispering in his ear, planting seeds, saying things like … "You're a powerful Master, You deserve your own slave …" he lapped it all up. He really believes the crap that I've been feeding him.' Max fixed Claudia with her cold gaze. 'I knew that my Mistress was going to find a new slave and so I prepared in advance, it could have been Natalie, you or anyone else - I was prepared.'

Claudia stared at her in amazement, 'And what now? You've exiled yourself from your Mistress. You've lost everything.'

Max shook her head, 'My Mistress will find us - but by then you will be damaged goods and she won't want you anymore.'

'Quite right. She won't want me,' Claudia sighed, 'but that's because she'll be too busy punishing you for what you've done. You're crazy.'

Max grew angry once more, 'And you've no idea what it means to be a slave … but you will, when Kelso and I break you, I promise.'

'She's right.'

Both women jumped at the sound of Kelso's voice and they both wondered, fearfully, how much he had heard. The look on his face said it all - he had heard everything. His anger was all for Max and the faintest hint of fear crossed the slave's eyes. He stared at her in silence, letting her know with his eyes exactly what he had heard - and right at that moment, for those few seconds when Kelso's fury was coldly directed at Max, he was more powerful than he had ever been before. He moved towards the slave, each step measured and deliberate. If he had just unleashed his fury, he would have lost that power. He must have realised that because he stood over the two women, not moving, not speaking, for several moments. His anger shone only in his eyes. He stared at Max and saw that glimmer of fear in her eyes. He made no reaction to it, he just turned and left, closing the door quietly behind him. The two women sat in silence, frozen, waiting for his return. It was both an eternity and a mere moment before the door opened again and Kelso entered the cell.

'Come here,' he ordered, his eyes on Claudia. She swallowed, too terrified to move but even more terrified to disobey. She started to climb to her feet but his voice cut the air, 'On your knees.' She fell onto all fours and crawled over to him. When she reached his feet she rested back on her ankles. Something slapped against her cheek and she flinched, expecting a strike.

'Take it.' Claudia looked up and realised that Kelso was holding the leather bra that she had pushed the tacks through. She lifted a shaking hand and took it from him.

'Put it on her.' Claudia thought that she had misheard him and she half looked up, caught in confusion. 'Put it on her,' Kelso growled, anger rolling through his words.

'On your knees.' Kelso ordered Max as Claudia crawled over to her. Max lifted herself onto her knees, moving easily despite the discomfort that she must have felt. Claudia slipped the bra straps over Max's hands and pushed them up her shoulders. Then she turned the vicious looking cups inwards to smother Max's breasts with the sharp points. 'Fasten it tightly.' Claudia shuffled on her knees until she was behind Max and then fastened the rear clasp. The back strap was adjustable and Claudia tightened it until the strap was cutting into the slave's skin. 'On your back,' Kelso ordered Max. When she was lying down, Kelso glared at Claudia, 'Sit on her face.'

Claudia moved slowly until she had her knees either side of Max's head. 'Put your cunt on her mouth.' She did so, giving a tiny shudder as Max's mouth pressed against her pussy lips. 'Now, lean forward, press down on her tits.' Claudia wanted to refuse but she feared the punishment more than she feared causing Max any discomfort. She bent forward, her stomach and ribs pressing down on Max's upper body. She put her hands on either side and was able to support her own weight. She didn't hear Kelso approach and gasped in surprise as her arms were suddenly wrenched behind her back. He snapped a pair of handcuffs around her wrists and then stepped back. Claudia was straining to keep her head up because the only other thing to do was to lower her face over the slave's pelvis. Her efforts were not helped by the hot gasps that escaped Max's lips. At any moment Claudia expected Kelso to tell her to lower her head but he didn't, instead he kicked Max's legs apart and knelt between her thighs. Claudia felt Max tense and she looked down to see Kelso attaching clamps to the slave's sensitive flesh. When he lifted three chains, Claudia had a good idea where those clamps had been attached. 'Open your mouth,' he commanded. Claudia did so, flinching as Kelso slipped the chains between her lips. 'Close.' She closed her mouth, biting down on the chains. 'If you let any one of those chains go, you'll be swapping places with the whore, understand?'

Claudia nodded and felt Max tense as the chains moved. 'Don't look so upset,' Kelso told Claudia. 'You should be happy, I'm going to let you come.' He kicked Max's thigh, 'Get started.' Claudia gasped and almost dropped the chains as Max's tongue suddenly probed between her cunt lips. Kelso stood and retrieved a thin cane from somewhere. He tapped the clamps at Max's pussy with the end of the cane and Claudia thought that he intended to beat her. That thought brought glowing warmth to Claudia's pussy and although she hated herself for it, she knew that Max could taste her pleasure. For an instant she was lost in the pleasure and closed her eyes. When she opened them again she realised that Kelso was gone. She had a moment to wonder where he had gone before the cane suddenly seared her buttocks. She gave a small cry, muffled by the chains, and her head lifted sharply. Max bucked underneath her, her hips rising off the floor in reaction to the violent tug on the clamps. The movement unbalanced Claudia and she had to press down against Max's body to steady herself. The slave gasped against her pussy, sending a shock of pleasure through her nerve endings. Another blow from the cane and they were both better prepared. Claudia managed to ease the tug on the clamps, which in turn eased Max's reaction. To start with Kelso's beating calmed the warm swelling at her pussy but soon enough the beating reached that glorious, pleasurable stage and Claudia was gasping against the chains in her mouth. It was a few moments later that she gushed into Max's mouth. Lost to her pleasure, she tossed her head and rode the slave's bucking that drew even more pleasure from her spasming pussy.

Chapter 2.10:

'Harder.' Kelso ordered.

Claudia tensed before she pulled on the chains, harder than before. The five chains, which she held in her fist hovering over Max's arched stomach, stretched out to meet the clamps attached to the slave's nipples, labia and clitoris. As she pulled on the chains the slave's bruised breasts stretched painfully tight, the nipples extended terribly. Claudia was sitting beside Max and was afforded a good view of the slave's features. Max's eyes were closed, her lips tightly shut too but there was a tension beneath that showed she was gritting her teeth. It was two days since Kelso had punished Max while she wore the studied bra and in that time he had taken every opportunity to involve Claudia in his puishment of the slave. Claudia had not disobeyed any of his commands to hurt Max, fearing her own punishment over Max's pain. But as the abuse continued, Claudia found the slave's reactions, or lack of, fascinating. And as Claudia hurt the slave more and more, she found herself wishing that she could be the one to draw a cry from the mute slave's lips instead of Kelso. If it started as a means to get one over on her new Master then that was soon forgotten as Claudia became lost in the challenge. If she felt any remorse, it was easily ignored when she remembered that it had been Max who had plotted to bring her here in the first place. But it wasn't a way to exact revenge, it was just a way to keep Kelso from hurting her. Claudia reasoned that if Kelso wasn't hurting her, then he wasn't breaking her.

She pulled harder on the chains without being ordered and felt a flutter of excitement when she saw Max's lips quiver. The slave had suffered so much, surely she couldn't take much more before a cry escaped those lips.

Claudia studied her carefully - maybe if Kelso were to get the leather belt … that thought froze her. What the hell was she doing? What the hell had happened to her? But once she had that thought about the studded belt there was no taking it back and, despite her best efforts, her mind was filled with images that made her nipples harden.

She was saved from these images by Kelso who moved round her to release Max's wrists and ankles that had been chained to the floor.

'On your hands and knees,' he ordered Claudia. She did so, lifting her head up as she knelt in front of him. His hard cock pressed against her cheek. 'You know what to do, whore.' She opened her mouth and let him slide in. He held the back of her head and pushed himself as far as he could go. She gagged and then relaxed, letting him slide into her throat. He had fucked her like this a lot and she was getting used to his deep invasion. 'Max,' Kelso said as a groan, 'make this slut come.' Claudia shivered as he said it, even before Max had touched her. With the chains still swinging from her breasts and cunt, Max moved in on Claudia. 'Fill her up.' Kelso groaned. Claudia gasped as she felt Max's fingers pushing between her labia and her body quivered as she was filled from both ends. Max's hand fucked her steadily, thrusting in and out as Kelso fucked her mouth. After a few moments Max slipped another finger in and then she pulled free to force all of her fingers into Claudia's wide cunt. Claudia groaned against the cock that thrust back and forth between her lips. Max bent her fingers to find that innermost sweet spot and Claudia cried out, choking on Kelso's cock.

'Hit her,' he commanded.

Claudia cried out, choking again as Max's palm slapped against her buttock. With one hand buried deep inside her, Max could only spank Claudia's left buttock but she hit it hard enough to make it burn. The heat radiated up her back and down her thighs. Max continued to tease her cunt as she slapped her arse and soon enough that heat quickly became focused between her legs. Claudia's entire body tensed and then shuddered uncontrollably as, whimpering against the cock that invaded her mouth, her orgasm seized her. The tremors of climax that rippled through her body were enough to send Kelso over the edge and he ejaculated deep into her throat. She choked again as he pulled free and she gasped, tears filling her pleasure-glazed eyes. She flopped forward, her body relaxing after the onslaught of her orgasm. Her shoulders heaved as she tried to regain her breath. Beneath the pleasurable tingling of her senses, her chest heaved and burned as hot as her stinging buttocks - but her climax had been too intense to be dampened by anything and she breathed heavily as her pussy continued to twitch and spasm.

'You like hurting her, don't you?'

Kelso's voice drifted to her from a long way off but she managed to answer, 'No.' Her voice sounded weak and pathetic. She cleared her throat and tried again, 'No.'

Kelso moved towards her and bent to slap his hand between her legs. 'Then why are you so wet?' he demanded.

She couldn't deny his words there was no point. Instead, she chose not to respond.

His lip curled into a crooked smile, 'Can't say I blame you for enjoying hurting her - not after everything she's done to you.'

Claudia's eyes narrowed, 'If that's true, imagine what I'd like to do to you.'

Kelso's eyes glinted. At first Claudia thought that it was anger but as she stared at him she realised that it

211

was arousal. 'So, you like it both ends of the whip,' she said.

'Seems I'm not the only one,' he responded as he licked her juice from his fingers.

'I'm not a Mistress,' Claudia announced firmly.

'Oh, I bet Mel would say different.'

Hearing Mel's name stunned Claudia into silence.

'That's right, I know all about you and Mel … and a certain Peter Strick.'

Claudia was annoyed by her surprise. She should have expected him to know - after all, Kelso had served Faith.

'I heard all about your little masquerade as her Mistress - only it wasn't quite the masquerade that you made out, was it? I bet you miss all that, don't you? And now Mel is back between Natalie's legs, tucked up safe in your little flat.' He sighed. 'God, you must just ache to go into their room at night, eh? You must be desperate to have a little fun with them. After all, you've earned it and I'd bet they'd thank you for it.'

Claudia stared at him in silence.

Kelso glanced at Max, 'Or if you prefer, Max is right there. She's all yours. Why don't you just let yourself go? You'll feel better for it.'

'Enough of the mind games, Kelso, you're not going to break me like that,' Claudia announced tiredly. 'You're not a thinker Kelso, you're a bully.'

He stared back, tight lipped, 'You've found some strength from somewhere, I like it, it means that you'll take more punishment.'

Claudia stared at Max. There was no denying that she had felt stronger since Kelso had turned on Max. Although she knew that the little strength that this had given her would not last for long and Max's continued hatred of her wasn't helping. If only Max would lay that hatred aside, maybe they could stand against Kelso. But

Max was more interested in seeing Claudia suffer than her own welfare. A look of despair must have shown in Claudia's eyes because Kelso's eyes glinted with near-triumph.

'You're almost mine,' he announced. 'But don't despair, once you're finally mine, I'll be tracking down a little companion for you.'

Claudia wanted to respond but Kelso turned and headed out of the room, locking the door behind him. When the door had closed, Claudia looked over at Max to see the slave half smiling, that same look of triumph in Max's eyes that she had seen in Kelso's. Claudia took a deep breath and closed her eyes in an attempt to block out the sight of the slave - but all she could see were two pairs of eyes that shone with triumph, their stare beating her back into the darkness. She felt a tear slide from the corner of her eye, others quickly followed.

'Cry all you like,' Max whispered. 'You'll be screaming again soon enough.'

Claudia wanted to shout at Max, to tell her to shut up, but she didn't have the strength.

'The sooner you accept what you are, the sooner you can appreciate and revel in your new life. All you have to do is submit.'

Submit, Claudia thought as sleep tugged at the edges of her consciousness. The thought of letting herself go, of giving herself over to those deep desires completely, made her pussy contract. She tried to ignore the spreading warmth as Max continued to dig away at the reserves of her strength.

Two more days passed, during which time Kelso appeared to tire of Max and turned his attentions back to Claudia. He still ordered Claudia to hurt Max, but Max was usually ordered to do the same. Claudia found it all the more terrible to hear her own cries after Max had suffered the same punishment in silence. In response to this, Claudia redoubled her efforts to make the slave scream but was only ever rewarded with silence and then even more pitiful cries of her own. Kelso must have noticed what was going on between the women because he let them loose on each other as often as their bodies could stand. He would always watch and always fuck one of them once he had enough of the entertainment. If he fucked Claudia, he always brought her to climax. When he fucked Max he always ordered that the slave pleasure Claudia while she was being mounted. More often than not, Max was left unsatisfied while Claudia's pain was followed by pleasure and it was getting harder to separate one from the other.

Claudia was sleeping, dreaming dark dreams and whimpering in her sleep. Even as her mind slept and dreamt, her body reacted to the images and her pussy moistened as her nipples hardened. She awoke half way through her dream-induced climax and groaned as she squeezed her thighs together, crushing her hand against her pussy lips.

'Enjoy that, did you?'

Claudia slowly opened her eyes and saw Max staring at her. She slowly sat up and looked around, searching for Kelso to see if he had seen her climax too.

'He's not here,' Max announced and moved a little closer. 'Do you know where he is?' She didn't wait for an answer. 'He's gone to that club again. He's going to find someone who will enjoy playing with you as much as he does.' The slave sniggered. 'In fact, I think he might even charge for the privilege. He's gonna make you into the proper little slut that you are.'

Claudia lifted her head to stare at the slave, but she didn't have the strength to convey her loathing fully.

'I can hear him coming,' Max smiled. 'I hope he's got Steve with him. You'll like Steve. He has a huge prick and he loves a piece of arse.'

'Yeah? Well maybe he'll fuck your arse too,' Claudia whispered.

'As long as he lubricates me with your juice, I'll be happy,' she smiled again as the sound of the door handle being turned echoed around them. 'You're weakening. You're succumbing. You're losing.'

Claudia looked at her and they locked stares.

'And if you're losing …' Max smiled. '… then I'm winning.'

'No, my little slave, you just lost.'

The female voice was like a rumble of thunder through the room.

'Mistress!' Max cried, flinging herself to the ground at Faith's feet. Faith snarled with anger and bent to grab a handful of the slave's hair, yanking her to her knees. 'I'm very disappointed in you,' she announced. She pushed the slave away and half turned to her male companions. 'Get them out of here.'

Claudia tried to shy away as one of the men approached. The movement caused pain to sear through her body and she collapsed to the cold floor. She felt the man's strong hands grip her and she gasped.

'Take it easy, you bastard. Hurt her and I'll hurt you.'

'Sorry, Mistress,' the man said but his voice sounded distant and Claudia closed her eyes as she drifted into unconsciousness.

She was awoken by a high-pitched scream and for a moment she thought that the scream had come from her own lips. She rolled onto her side and tried to crawl away. Hands touched her shoulders and she cried out.

'It's okay. It's okay.'

Claudia recognised the voice and let a gasp escape her lips, 'Mel?'

Both women jumped as another scream echoed through the room.

'Where's that coming from?' Claudia whispered.

'I don't know,' Mel replied softly as she studied Claudia.

They sat in silence for several minutes. Eventually Mel started to say something but was stopped by the door opening.

'Well now, you look better.' Faith smiled as she closed the door behind her.

Despite everything that had happened, Claudia was still warmed by the sight of her. She realised now that, whatever was between them, it would never fade.

'What do you want?' Claudia asked nervously.

'I just wanted to see you before you went.'

'You're letting me go?' Claudia asked.

'Of course,' Faith smiled. 'You're not my prisoner, Claudia.'

'And I'm not your slave,' Claudia announced, combating the look that she saw in Faith's eyes.

'You're as bound to me as Max is.'

'Where is Max?' Claudia asked, sidestepping Faith's comment.

Faith glanced towards the next room, 'I'm teaching her the error of her ways. Would you like to watch?'

Claudia shook her head firmly, she had no desire to

see what Faith was doing to make the trained, silent slave scream so terribly.

'Then it's time for you to go,' Faith announced.

Claudia stood slowly, allowing Mel to support her. 'Tell me it's over, Faith.'

The mistress frowned.

'This whole thing with you and Natalie. I kept my end of the deal, now you keep yours.'

Faith smiled, 'Even after everything you've been through, you're still thinking of others.'

'Is it over?' Claudia whispered.

'It's over - I'll let Natalie go, now that I've found you again.'

'There's no need for us to ever see each other again, Faith. I can't live in your world.'

'You already are,' Faith responded. 'And when you realise that, you'll come to find me and I'll be waiting.'

'No.'

'Yes. There is history between us, my love, and our history will chain us together … forever.'

Claudia stared at her, she wanted to deny the young mistress' words but she couldn't. No more than she could deny the warm glow at her pussy caused by the very thought of succumbing to Faith. It was quickly becoming clear that it wasn't a case of whether Claudia would finally fall into Faith's dark embrace. But when.

Dark Surrender

By Kim Knight

Leigh Goldman, a young psychotherapist is disturbed and strangely fascinated by Mel, a young girl who calmly relates to her, her experiences of harsh sexual dominance at the hands of her master. Leigh has never come across the world of SM and is soon out of her depth as she desperately tries to help Mel escape from her slavery.

First she must find who the strange and sinister master is, then she must convince him that she is a dominant too. But most importantly she has to explore her own sexuality to the very limits and that leads her into darker and stranger places than she could ever have imagined.

Kim Knight makes an impressive debut in Dark Surrender. It is intended as the first of a series of self-contained novels under the collective title; 'Unchained'.

A Slave's Desire

By Kim Knight

Mel, recently freed from slavery, is determined to win her lover's freedom. But Natalie is still a slave and has been sold into slavery in Russia. Helped by the mysterious Claudia, Mel tracks her but is foiled at the last minute.

The vicious mistress' called 'Faith' has had the beautiful Natalie taken to a training camp in Algeria. Here her torment seems never-ending and she sinks into complete submission.

Inventive, cruel and clever; Kim Knight's second volume in the 'Unchained' series is as absorbing as it is highly erotic.

CONTROLLING CATHERINE

By ELENA GREGORY

A minor burglary leads Catherine into a meeting with a very dominant policeman and before she knows what's happening, she finds herself falling under his spell. But she doesn't slip easily into the role of submissive and some strange adventures lie in store for her before she finally comes to terms with being controlled.

Elena Gregory gives her readers a fascinating glimpse into the secret world of the submissive woman in this, her second Silver Moon novel.

DARKER DREAMS

by TESSA VALMUR

Lara Lustral is beautiful, wealthy and bored. The only place where she can find the action she craves is the Dreamscape Institute. The year is 2027 and at the institute you can actually live out your most secret fantasies.

But when your secret fantasies are as erotic as Lara's are and the enigmatic Dr Mackennan is watching everything........the Institute is not a safe place to be! Lara finds out that the reality of submission is a lot harder than she had ever dreamed.

LADY NIGHTSHADE

BY FRANCINE WHITTAKER

Kenny Phillips does not like dominant women. Not any more. Not since his Mistress betrayed him. But when he follows up rumours about strange goings on in a remote castle in Spain, he finds out that his resolve is not quite as firm as he thought.

Through Mistress Celandine, Mistress Angelica, Mistresas Foxglove and most deadly of all, Lady Nightshade, he is brought to a full understanding of his place in life.

Now firmly established as one of the foremost erotic authoresses currently writing, Francine Whittaker again serves up a cruel, ingenious and spellbinding tale of dominant females and their male slaves.

THE CONTRACT

BY SARAH FISHER

When Emily Lawrence signs away her body to pay off her lover's debt, she steps into the dark, compelling world of pain and passion. In a luxurious, isolated mansion Emily discovers her true nature. Sold to the highest bidder and branded, she finds herself caught up in the seductive world of submission and domination.

Once signed, there is no getting out of *The Contract* and obedience, pain and desire are all part of it.

Silver Moon have over a hundred titles of erotic domination and submission in their catalogue. If you would like to find out more and join our readers' club absolutely free, then write to:

Silver Moon Readers' Services
The Shadowline Building
Wembley Street
Gainsborough
Lincs DN21 2AJ
Tel: 01427 816710 (during office hours)

You will receive a free quarterly magazine with features, interviews, news, views and special offers plus the chance to order titles which are only available to club members.

Alternatively you can log onto:
www.adultbookshops.com